"You have luscious lips, Trina, know that?" Sam said, his mouth deserting hers, leaving her breathless and needy.

Her head moved from side to side because she couldn't speak.

"That first night, at my house, you licked them. I wanted to do it too. I hated wanting it, especially so fast, and I fought it."

His breath grazed her ear like a warm mist. "I know," she murmured, wondering if she would be able to continue her own fight. The security of his embrace was so tempting.

"But these . . ." He lifted the hand that she had curled around his biceps and brought it to his mouth. "These are what drive me out of my mind." His parted lips skimmed lightly over the top of her hand before turning it to leave a lingering kiss on her palm. "They're so soft."

He took her hands and was moving them over his face, touching all those sharp angles and delectable curves she'd longed to explore. "What do soft hands matter?" she murmured.

She felt the vibration in his throat, a cross between a laugh and a groan. "You wouldn't ask if you could peek into my fantasies. Believe me, soft hands play an important part in those."

"Sam," Trina said, attempting to pull her hands away but ending up with her palms splayed against his chest. "We both know this will lead to big trouble."

"Honey, it already has. I've just decided not to fight it anymore. . . ."

WHAT ARE *LOVESWEPT* ROMANCES?

They are stories of true romance and touching emotion. We believe those two very important ingredients are constants in our highly sensual and very believable stories in the *LOVESWEPT* line. Our goal is to give you, the reader, stories of consistently high quality that may sometimes make you laugh, sometimes make you cry, but are always fresh and creative and contain many delightful surprises within their pages.

Most romance fans read an enormous number of books. Those they truly love, they keep. Others may be traded with friends and soon forgotten. We hope that each *LOVESWEPT* romance will be a treasure—a "keeper." We will always try to publish

LOVE STORIES YOU'LL NEVER FORGET
BY AUTHORS YOU'LL ALWAYS REMEMBER

The Editors

Loveswept® 548

Linda Jenkins
Mr. Wonderful

BANTAM BOOKS
NEW YORK · TORONTO · LONDON · SYDNEY · AUCKLAND

MR. WONDERFUL

A Bantam Book / June 1992

*If you would be interested in receiving protective vinyl
covers for your Loveswept books, please write to this address
for information:*

Loveswept
Bantam Books
P.O. Box 985
Hicksville, NY 11802

ISBN 0-553-44181-7

Published simultaneously in the United States and Canada

*Bantam Books are published by Bantam Books, a division of
Bantam Doubleday Dell Publishing Group, Inc. Its trademark,
consisting of the words "Bantam Books" and the portrayal of
a rooster, is Registered in U.S. Patent and Trademark Office
and in other countries. Marca Registrada. Bantam Books, 666
Fifth Avenue, New York, New York 10103.*

PRINTED IN THE UNITED STATES OF AMERICA

OPM   0 9 8 7 6 5 4 3 2 1

Mr. Wonderful

One

"For someone who couldn't wait for me to get here, you sure are a hard man to track down."

Katarina Bartok frowned, immediately wishing she'd chosen a different opening line. The ax-wielding giant on the other side of her car looked more annoyed than pleased by her arrival. And a single glance at his bare, muscular chest kept the words "hard man" resounding inside her brain.

"That's why I live in these woods." With one stroke of his massive arms, he buried the blade in a fat oak log. "If I want to see someone, *I* do the tracking down."

He let go of the vibrating ax handle and, like a gunslinger primed for a showdown, came toward her in a slow stalk. After a quick check of her license plate, he said, "You're a ways from home, Miss New York. What brings you to Missouri?"

Trina retreated a step. At five feet nine she stood on fairly equal footing with the average male.

There was, however, nothing average about this one, and she had to look up to meet his light green eyes. "I'm on my way out West. Lake of the Ozarks is just a stopover."

He crossed powerful, tendon-laced forearms in front of a narrow torso and rocked back on the heels of scarred rawhide boots. His gaze flicked up, then down, lingering a heartbeat longer than it took to measure her full height. "A stopover, huh? Then you made a wrong turn somewhere."

A light bulb went off in Trina's head, and she smiled. He'd mistaken her for a tourist who'd gotten lost. "No wrong turn. I'm Katarina Bartok. Trina." She offered her hand. "The desk clerk at Chimera Lodge gave me directions."

Cool green eyes narrowed as anger replaced annoyance. "They know better than to send anybody to my house."

Since he ignored the hand, she let it fall to her side. Trina was certain she hadn't misunderstood Robert Wonder's instructions about how to locate his son. "They were only following your father's orders. He sent a note that said you were expecting me and that I should come here if you weren't at the lodge."

"My father?" One brow quirked, as if he was skeptical. "What's he have to do with this?"

Was the man dense or merely forgetful? "I was with your parents last night in St. Louis. He called to tell you about me, that I'd be driving in sometime today. According to him, you wanted me as soon as possible."

Sam Wonder loomed over her, casting a long shadow in the setting sun. He smelled hot. Not sweaty. Hot. Deep inside, unexpected warmth flooded Trina. A primal feminine instinct compelled her to get closer. Common sense made her back away farther.

"Dad told you that, did he? That I *wanted* you?"

She hadn't realized a hoarse voice could sound quite so interesting, so . . . desirable. The warmth spread to her cheeks. "That's what he said."

Sam planted one hand on the roof of her car, the other on his hip. "And why, since I've never heard of Katarina Bartok, am I supposedly so anxious for you to arrive?"

"Never heard of me? That's impossible! Didn't you speak with your father last night? Around ten o'clock?"

"I did. We discussed the weather and crappie fishing. He asked if I had any out-of-town trips scheduled. I reminded him about the Memorial Day barbecue in a couple of weeks, talked about this season's bookings and some other company-related things."

"But he didn't mention—"

"Ms. Bartok and her imminent arrival? Afraid not."

For a few seconds Trina was speechless. Then a sinking sensation hit her. This ill-fated detour to the Ozarks was turning out to be as big a disappointment as everything else she'd attempted during the past month.

She had jumped at the temporary assignment because it would give her a chance to regroup. Each day she'd become more afraid that her search was a fool's errand. It had crossed her mind that she ought to turn around and go home.

Except she no longer had a home. Or a family. Or much of anything else.

She did, nevertheless, still have her professional skills. "Then you aren't planning an expansion project for your resort? You don't need a consultant to advise you about the financial options for such a venture? And you didn't authorize your father to hire me?"

"I *am* planning, and I *do* need. But I didn't authorize him to hire *anyone*." His stiffened spine made him appear even taller. "Dad plays no part in what goes on around here, and he had no business implying that he does."

Stubbornness displaced Trina's disappointment. Sam Wonder had a job opening, even if he hadn't aimed for her to fill it. But that was something she could change his mind about.

"During the drive I started thinking ahead, planning. Would you like to hear my list of suggestions?"

His seemingly perpetual scowl deepened. "Save your breath. I'm not in the market for any suggestions from Dad's viewpoint."

Unprepared for hostility, Trina felt her confidence sink another notch. She compensated by trying too hard to impress Sam Wonder with her qualifications. "I have hundreds of contacts, sources of financing all over the country. International connections too."

"Look, Ms. Bartok, I'm not sure exactly what your angle is, but whatever you're selling, I'm not buying."

"Just give me a chance. Your father described what you need, and I can provide it."

Now he seemed more than suspicious. In fact, he looked downright incensed. "I think I'm getting the picture. How well do you know Dad?"

Trina unclenched her fingers. She had come here expecting to meet a successful businessman and immerse herself in work. Instead, she'd landed on the doorstep of a half-naked log-splitter with world-class pecs, impressive shoulders, and a bad attitude, none of which were on her agenda. She fervently wished he would put on a shirt.

"I met Robert about six years ago at a bankers' conference, and we became long-distance friends. He's referred several clients to me for trust and estate planning. In turn, I steered some investors his way."

"Are you saying it was only business?"

She bristled at his inference. "Of course it was business! Your father is never less than a perfect gentleman," she asserted, implying that Sam suffered by comparison. "When he found out I'd be driving cross-country, he insisted I visit him and his wife in St. Louis."

Sam nodded, apparently comprehending something she had missed. "Which you did last night."

"Yes," Trina said, wishing she could get hold of Robert and sort out the situation.

"Did he ever mention he had a son?"

She thought back over the numerous conversations she'd had with Sam's father. "He might have mentioned one in passing, though I don't recall anything specific. For certain, last night was the first time I'd heard your name."

His forehead creased with obvious disbelief, and

he shook his head. "So he actually did try to lure you here with the pretense of a job?"

Trina couldn't stifle an exasperated huff. She was tired of being grilled about imaginary transgressions. "What other reason would there be for sending me?"

"Come on now, it's not like this is an original idea. Did you really think I wouldn't catch on to something so transparent?"

Through gritted teeth she said, "I don't know what you're talking about."

His smile was neither pleasant nor friendly. "I'm talking about matchmaking. As in Dad trying to marry off his only child. As in assuring himself of a grandchild or two. Must have given up on the home-grown variety if he's getting desperate enough to import someone from out of state."

Dumbfounded, she gaped at Sam. It had never entered her mind to suspect Robert of such an underhanded trick. She felt like a gullible idiot. "Matchmaking! But I—But you—We . . ." Palms up, Trina gestured helplessly.

Sam studied her for a long time. "Either you're a damn good actress or you're not any happier about this than I am. Are you really shocked?"

What she was, was mortified. Knowing that she, too, was a victim of the devious ruse didn't make the situation any more bearable. "I think this is my cue for a clever exit line, but to be honest, words fail me."

He shifted restlessly, avoiding eye contact. At last he said, "Look, I'm sorry Dad sent you down here on a wild-goose chase. The least I can do is offer you a room at the lodge tonight. And dinner."

"That isn't necessary. None of this is your fault."

"I know. But somehow I feel responsible."

Trina could understand that. She'd been *responsible* all her life. "Don't give it another thought. I'm terribly sorry for bothering you." Failure and humiliation were closing in on her. She wanted to run. "I'll be on my way."

"I insist. And I guarantee you won't find better accommodations or food anywhere in the area."

"No doubt." She'd only been at Chimera a short time, yet it was long enough for her to see that it was a luxurious, superbly run operation. "But I've already imposed on you enough."

"Not half as much as Dad's imposed on you." He slid a watch from a jeans pocket.

She caught herself staring at the denim that molded his hips and . . . Heaven forbid! That wasn't on her agenda either. She whirled around, feigning interest in the exterior of his stone and stained-wood house. Just enough trees had been cleared to make room for the structure and the small, well-landscaped yard, giving it the appearance of a natural hideaway.

"Let's go inside."

Sam's suggestion derailed her wayward train of thought. She turned back to him. "Why?"

"If we're going to dinner, I need a shower." One hand passed through his dark blond hair and swiped over his damp skin.

She watched his fingers comb through the fine dusting of hair that spanned his upper chest. Her mouth dried up, her pulse rate surged. "Maybe I'd better wait here."

"Temperature's real high about now."

Her gaze collided with his. What she saw there had nothing to do with the thermometer reading. "It has to cool off soon." Her words came out breathless, expectant. "I mean, the sun's almost gone."

He nodded. His eyes closed for a few seconds. "Come on, Kat-a-rina."

His voice was soft, but unrelenting, and her will to protest suddenly deserted her. Silent, she walked with him to the door.

From the entry hall she saw that the house angled up three levels, probably to take advantage of the sheer hillside overlooking the lake. His furnishings were spartan, the decor uncluttered and very masculine.

"Cold drinks in the fridge. Help yourself," he said, directing her toward the kitchen. "Give me twenty minutes."

As Trina's eyes tracked him up the stairs she added salivating over Sam Wonder to her list of recent lapses. Of course, it didn't compare to quitting her job, doing away with most of her possessions, and squandering her money on a flashy car when she hadn't even known how to drive.

Had her father been alive, he would have hung his head in despair, as if his daughter's foolishness wounded him. A smile of bittersweet recollection touched her lips. Anton Bartok was gone now, leaving a legacy of mixed blessings.

She knew for certain that this trip to California would have infuriated him. He'd have done everything in his power to prevent her from making it.

"Anthony chose to go away, Trina. You must forget you ever had a brother."

She had struggled to be obedient and accept her father's decree, mainly because each passing year seemed to reinforce Anton's assertion that Tony wanted nothing more to do with her. But in the fifteen years that had elapsed, there had not been a single day when she hadn't thought of him.

It took Sam closer to a half hour to clean up. He'd taken the time to shave again, though he wasn't sure why he'd gone to the trouble. This wasn't the kind of date where he was trying to impress a woman. In fact, it wasn't a date at all. More like . . . an obligation. Yeah, right.

He'd come down on her pretty hard when she'd tried to convince him to give her the job. At first he had seen her appearance as one more example of his father's well-meant interference in his business affairs, and no way could he have let that slide. But no one was good enough to fake her reaction to the matchmaking.

He found her looking at the lake through the glass living-room wall, arms wrapped around her middle. Pretty. She was that, yet the word didn't say enough. Tall and leggy, with lots of walnut-colored hair, dark amber eyes, and dusky skin, she could pass for a model. The exotic, glamourous type. Magazine-cover and male-fantasy material.

It bothered him to notice so many details. And to feel the edgy awareness she stirred in him, like nerves too close to the surface. Sam had figured thirty-seven was old enough for his hormones to have peaked and gone into decline. Apparently he'd counted himself out too soon.

So he liked what he saw. Big deal. Hadn't his ex-wife always said a man wasn't a man if he didn't look? While he was married, he'd never wanted to. With only a few exceptions in the ten years since he'd been single again, looking was pretty much all he had trusted himself to do.

"Kat-a-rina?" He rolled her name off his tongue the way she'd said it, and savored the musical flow.

"Oh," she said, half turning. "I didn't hear you come down."

Because she'd been preoccupied. "That's me, quiet as a mouse."

"'Mouse' doesn't come to mind when I think of you. 'Lion,' maybe. Or 'stallion.'" She looked appalled, her cheeks turning the shade of her raspberry silk dress before she faced the window again. "I didn't mean—"

Sam heard a low rumble in his throat and masked it with a cough. Why did his father have to spring this on him now? He had his life arranged just the way he wanted it. And yet, he'd insisted that she stay, when he ought to have sent her packing.

"Your view is spectacular. Water and trees and not a sign of civilization as far as the eye can see."

She was reaching, seeking a way to ease the tension. It didn't work. Even her voice, with its faintly European accent, got under his skin and inside his head, whispering of hot midnights and tangled sheets. He moved to share the view. To smell her perfume. "Yeah," he said, his voice hoarser than usual, "I don't think I'll ever get tired of looking . . . at the water."

She reached to touch the glass, as if she could draw the outdoors closer. "There's so much space here, and it's so quiet. Very different from what I'm used to."

Sam knew all about what city women, with their aspirations and pretensions to sophistication, were used to. "I'm sure this place is a mite remote and rustic for your taste," he drawled. "And I suppose the people seem equally quaint and provincial."

"Isn't it a mite condescending of you to haul out your phony country twang and try to label me a big-city snob?"

"I wasn't aware of trying to do that."

She pinned him with those clear, compelling eyes. "I don't believe you, Sam Wonder. I think you're aware of everything and everyone you come into contact with."

He damn sure was aware of her. Painfully so. There was powerful stuff going on between them, a complication he didn't need and didn't want. "Let's get out of here," he said abruptly.

She didn't reply, but seemed as relieved as Sam to be back outside. She drew a deep breath and gestured to his Bronco in the drive. "How about you lead and I follow?"

A smart man would have pounced on the chance to put a lot of space between them. "How about I ride with you?"

"You won't have a way to get back. Afterward." She licked her lips.

An invitation? *No way, you moron.* All the same,

he wanted to lick them too. "I'll, uh, bring one of the lodge's boats. I do that sometimes. It's faster."

"Whatever you say." She gave the Bronco another look before leading the way to the Porsche. "Sorry it's so crowded." She transferred a stack of books, maps, and papers to her lap so he could wedge his six-four frame into the passenger seat. "It's okay to put your feet on those bags. If they'll fit."

They did, barely, with about two square inches to spare. "No offense, but I'm glad this is yours and not mine. I don't think I'd be able to stand up after several thousand miles in it."

She considered that a moment before twisting the key. "Want to know the truth? If I had it to do over, I'd go for something more user-friendly than a sports car." She sighed. "I hate to admit this, but I think a nice, roomy station wagon would better suit my style."

Uh-uh, Sam corrected silently. Definitely not a station wagon. A luxury import, maybe, all sleek and polished and lush on the inside. He groaned. His knees clunked against the dashboard.

"Sorry," she repeated, and ground into first gear. "Belligerent Teutonic monster," she muttered under her breath as the car roared and shot forward, spitting gravel in all directions.

Sam fastened his seat belt and watched her do battle with the clutch and transmission. But he quickly forgot auto parts and stared at her hands, cursing himself for not touching them when she'd given him the chance. They looked cloud-soft and capable of taking a man to heaven. After fifteen minutes of silent torture the lodge was a welcome sight.

"Pull up under the portico." He could already see a pair of young bellhops ogling the showy red car. "I'll have someone park it."

Trina braked to a shuddering stop, a fitting finale. She chewed on her bottom lip and rested one hand on a carton lodged between the seats. "I'd rather not let anyone . . ." She made a small encompassing gesture. "All this . . ."

"No problem. We'll leave it right here. Bring the keys with you." He opened the door and disentangled himself from the low seat. "Keep an eye on this, Rob," he told one of the college boys on duty.

"Sure thing, Mr. Wonderful!"

Sam glared at him, but it was wasted. Rob was taking his duties very seriously, opening Trina's door, helping her get out, smiling in welcome.

She came around the car to join him, a wistful smile softening her expression. "Mr. Wonderful?"

He winced. "I thought I was being so clever to name the corporation Wonderful! Never guessed I'd get stuck with that stupid nickname."

"It isn't stupid. It's . . . wonderful." She paused just outside the double doors. "Sam, for the last time, please don't feel obligated to look after me. I can take care of a meal and a room on my own. Don't think you have to atone for your father's sins. You needn't go overboard."

Sam had a disturbing premonition he was about to do just that. Go overboard with sins of his own, and make a colossal fool of himself in the process.

Trina entered the lobby ahead of Sam, the lyrics and melody of an old tune teasing her memory.

She hadn't heard it in years, but could distinctly recall her parents dancing to it amid the clutter of their cramped Brooklyn apartment. A scratchy phonograph record had provided their accompaniment, and her mother always sang along with the words of her favorite song. To Oma Bartok, Anton had been her very own "Mr. Wonderful."

Here, now, it was an eerie twist of fate to encounter a man who went by the same name. A man who inspired such tempestuous feelings and reactions within her that she knew she'd never be able to swallow a bite of dinner.

She made a quick stop at the ladies' lounge to splash cool water on her face, slather her hands with lotion, and give herself a stern talking-to. After that, she was able to sit across a table from Sam and keep up a continuous flow of small talk while working her way through an excellent trout specialty. All in all, Trina was feeling quite confident that she had shaken her immediate and exaggerated fascination with Sam. When he excused himself, she sipped a second cup of cappuccino, celebrating her speedy recovery. Then he reappeared, so tall, so breathtakingly masculine, and she had to look up into those green eyes that reminded her of willow leaves in spring.

"How about it? Ready to go to your room?" A key in his hand and the resonance in his voice made it sound like the most intimate of questions.

Ignoring the faint trembling of her fingers, she said, "Ready," then had to clear her throat against the unexpected huskiness. Trina wasn't naive. Sam was not the first man she'd been attracted to. But it had never happened this fast. And it had never felt as though she were hurtling off a cliff at a hundred miles an hour.

Maybe it was a blessing that the job hadn't panned out. She didn't need a distraction like Sam Wonder when her future was so uncertain that she didn't know where she'd be tomorrow, much less in a month.

Rising, she groped for her purse. "I intended to see about getting a room before now. Somehow time got away."

Sam bypassed the registration desk and ushered her out the main entrance. "It's taken care of."

She pulled to a halt and said very distinctly, "I would feel much better if you had let me handle this myself." Determined to take charge of her life, Trina realized she was overly sensitive about anyone doing anything that smacked of an attempt to control her. Especially someone like Sam, whose very presence agitated her.

"And I would feel much better if you'd stop making such a big deal of dinner and a night on the house. We covered this ground earlier."

Trina suppressed the urge to tell him to mind his own business, that she could look after herself. Sam was only being generous. Couldn't she accept it graciously? "I suppose one night can't do any harm."

"No, it can't. So let's get you tucked in."

It was just a figure of speech, Trina knew. Still, the image of Sam doing the job personally stayed with her all the way to the car.

"I had them put you in the Pavilion. It has the

newest rooms and the best view of sunrise over the lake."

By now, Trina was counting the hours until morning came and she could make her escape. She had to push and get to California as quickly as possible. A month on the road, followed by the disaster here, had taught her one thing about herself. She was not cut out for a life of idleness.

Spending money when none was coming in had driven her into a near frenzy of insecurity. The proceeds from her father's insurance money in the bank and her hidden stash of emergency funds weren't enough to reassure her. Trina needed a job, and she'd have to move on to find one.

She gripped the wheel and followed Sam's directions, steering the bucking car along a winding, hilly drive toward an annex a short distance from the main lodge. First gear wasn't going so smoothly, so she scraped into second.

"Ever thought of trading up to an automatic transmission?" he inquired, one palm braced on the dash.

"According to the salesman, you can't be one with the power and excitement of a high-strung racing animal unless you have a firm hand on the stick."

His harsh intake of air seemed to steal her share of oxygen. She looked at him and saw that his eyes, focused on her right hand and illuminated in the eerie light of the dashboard, had turned primal, wild. "What is it? What's wrong?"

Teeth bared, he threw his head back, as if in pain. His hips twisted on the seat. "Nothing," he growled, closing his eyes. "Just drive."

She did, though Sam's odd behavior made her clumsier. She couldn't imagine what she'd said or done to provoke his outburst.

"Park here." He pointed to a stone retaining wall.

Neither could vacate the car fast enough. In a flurry of nervous activity Trina lifted a small suitcase from the rear deck, then went around and claimed her cosmetic pouch from behind the passenger seat. Raising the front hood, she removed a duffel, a tote, a cardboard hatbox, and added them to the stack. The portable file? Yes, better not leave her important papers behind.

"Sure you don't need anything else?"

She didn't mind being a source of amusement. Anything to jar him out of the strange mood. "Traveling with so little space requires creative packing. Lots of small bundles stow easier than big pieces of luggage."

"But is all this stuff necessary for one night?"

Trina paused to survey the growing pile. "Um, yes, I'm afraid so." These meager parcels contained the few precious treasures from her past that she had kept, and she clung to them, surrounded herself with them as if they provided both solace and salvation. "I need them all."

Sam shrugged, picked up some of the gear, and tucked more under his arms. "You're the boss."

Muttering to herself, she grabbed a plastic supermarket bag out of the spare-tire well. From under the driver's seat she palmed a red-and-white can and chucked it into the bag. But not quickly enough.

Forestalling his question, she explained, "Survival rations. Never leave home without them.

Can't tell where you might get stranded." For example, a posh resort with five restaurants and twenty-four-hour room service.

He was eyeing her with the kind of suspicion usually reserved for escaped felons. "You have athelete's foot?"

Trina looked down, startled to see what she had just removed from the side-door compartment. She had planned to slip out later to collect the rest. "Yes. That is, no." She buried the can beneath her pseudo-soup. "It's . . . preventive medicine."

"I see."

He clearly didn't, but she wasn't about to reveal what she stored in her bogus containers. Might as well go for it, she decided, reaching under and behind the steering wheel to liberate the final can.

"Is the STP for medicinal purposes also?"

"Of course not. I use this on the car. To, uh"— she squinted at the label in the lamplight—"clean carbs and injectors." She gave Sam credit for not quizzing her on the finer details of carbs and injectors, whatever they were.

"That should do it," she announced, making busywork out of locking the doors and gathering her share of the baggage. "Ready when you are." As if he hadn't been standing here all that time weighted down like a pack mule.

When they reached the door, he had to put down his load to dig for the key he'd pocketed. He was being remarkably stoic about lugging in so much paraphernalia. "Drop it on the bed," she said. "I'll rearrange it later."

The room was large and attractive, its furnishings a cut above standard hotel decor, as was everything else about Chimera. She was impressed with what she'd seen and curious about how he'd got started in the resort business. But those were just a few of the questions she had about Sam Wonder, questions doomed to go unanswered because after tonight she'd never see him again.

Trina told herself it was for the best. He made her feel vulnerable and receptive and a lot of other things that were dangerous.

She put the width of the king-size bed between them before speaking. "I want to thank you for your hospitality. You've been more than generous."

Pensive, Sam looked at her. "I've been thinking . . ." He frowned and shook his head. "Never mind. I'll pick you up for breakfast in the morning."

She wanted to accept as badly as she needed to refuse. "What time?" So much for prudence.

"Eight." After he had opened the door, he turned around. "Kat-a-rina?"

"Yes," she whispered, trying not to respond to the thickening of his voice and the shivers he generated just by saying her name that special way.

"Lock the door behind me."

Breath suspended in her throat, she only stared at him until he ordered, "Do it now!"

She crossed the room like a sleepwalker, and as much for support as to do his bidding, curved her fingers around edge of the door . . . an instant before Sam's hand claimed the same spot, covering hers, squeezing.

The sizzle when they touched was imaginary. Had to be.

The heat was not.

Two

She had spent the night in Sam Wonder's bed.

Trina hugged her pillow, then opened her eyes and surveyed the room. Sam Wonder's bed, all right. Technically. But he had shared it only in her dreams. "A dream is not the same as a wish," she asserted with bravado.

As memories of their brief but volatile touch washed over her, she flung back the sheet, her body much too warm to tolerate cover. The contact had shocked them. She'd gasped, "Oh!" and Sam's guttural "Unh!" sounded as if he had taken a punch. Both had recoiled.

By this morning she could no longer delude herself that the electricity was imaginary.

She bounded out of bed and headed straight for the shower. If she hurried, she could pack the car, leave a thank-you message for Sam at the desk, and be on the road before eight. A trifle rude, she admitted, but etiquette wasn't her top priority.

Besides, he would probably be more relieved than upset by her untimely departure.

His change of attitude and insistence on her staying might mean that he'd decided she wasn't part of Robert's plot after all. But by leaving early, she could spare them both the embarrassment of having to deal with it again.

Trina soaped herself with ruthless vigor, as if she could scrub away all recollections of Sam Wonder and the high-voltage energy he generated. It had the opposite effect, making her skin even more sensitized.

When they were together, simmering undercurrents made them skittish, like animals circling and testing each other. They seemed to be saying one thing while thinking another. Nuances belying their words made simple conversation a strain.

She grabbed a towel and dried off hastily. No, she didn't need this kind of aggravation. Not when she had so many miles to go, literally and figuratively.

She stepped into a denim jumpsuit and fastened a belt of silver medallions around her waist. Before she'd finished pulling her hair back with a clip, she heard two raps on the door. It was Sam. The feathery sensation at the base of her spine told her so.

She fumbled with the locks, irritated that her awkwardness made opening the door a difficult chore.

"Kat-a-rina."

One word and his just-out-of-bed voice had her stomach doing acrobatics. "You're early."

"I woke up hungry."

He looked born hungry. *Oh, Lord. Move, Trina.*

Don't let him touch you again. Dashing about the room, she collected her purse and the plastic shopping bag that contained her phony canned goods, then hung a Do Not Disturb sign on the door before closing it behind them. "I'll come back and load the rest after we eat. That way I won't detain you."

"There's nothing that won't wait. Anybody here will tell you I don't operate on a set schedule."

"I know what you mean. The day I dumped my business suits at the church thrift shop, I swore I'd stop being a slave to the clock or the calendar." And to someone else's plans. But this trip had taught her that old habits died hard and freedom wasn't all it was cracked up to be.

Sam indicated a serpentine walkway bisecting a Japanese garden. Bordered with beds of peonies and multicolored begonias, it sloped gently upward to the main building where the restaurants were.

"So, to escape the rut, you chose to go out West. That covers a lot of territory. Anywhere specific?"

If only she knew. "I guess I'll start in California, around L.A." That covered a lot of territory too.

"You have family or friends there? A job?"

All of the above, she hoped. "No, nothing. Yet." Trina hesitated, self-conscious about how tentative she sounded. "I have to take care of some unfinished business with my father's estate." That was true, as far as it went. "But I've been thinking about staying on, maybe starting over."

"Yeah, well, sometimes that's all we can do."

Had experience put the resignation in his tone? What had gone wrong with his life that he'd needed to start over? When had it happened? Put a lid on the questions, she ordered herself. His psyche and his past were not her concerns. All she needed to worry about was getting through the next hour. "How long have you been at Chimera?"

"Counting the time it took to plan and build, close to ten years."

"It must have been successful from the beginning. Your father told me this will be your third expansion." Trina cautioned herself not to lament the small role she was to have played in the project.

Sam bent to pluck a weed, the single intruder in an otherwise perfectly tended flower bed. More evidence of a tight ship. "Luck and timing played a big part in our success. We were set to open just as the demand for a more complete type of resort arose."

"Some might attribute it to smart planning rather than good timing or luck."

"Whatever. Population here has quadrupled in the last decade, along with a boom in tourism. People pour in from all over." He pointed a finger at her. "Even New York."

Trina held up both hands in mock surrender. In this idyllic atmosphere of rockeries, man-made brooks, and exotic blossoms, she could almost relax. "You sound like a chamber-of-commerce booster."

"I guess I am. The lodge does work closely with the chamber, trying to promote our area for conventions and corporate functions, especially in winter." He paused to test the water in a lily pond. "Florida in February, this isn't. We have to appeal to a different market."

Though he hadn't asked, Trina couldn't stop from volunteering her ideas for selling Chimera in winter. "Target those who can drive here within a few hours. Offer them a very attractive room rate, plus some giveaways. Maybe free massages, two-for-one dinners, discounts in the shops. Establish a couple of special events at the same time every year to encourage repeat business."

His brows rose in surprise. "I thought you said your field is trust and estate planning."

"It is—was. At the bank. But I double-majored in accounting and finance, and I also have an MBA. Which only means that I know a little about a lot of things relating to money." Trina cringed. Her speech smacked of singles-mixer chitchat, self-importance disguised as self-deprecation.

"Then you *could* do the job Dad allegedly sent you for?"

"I'd never have agreed to come if I weren't qualified." She gave him a rueful smile. "It goes without saying that I wouldn't have come at all if I had known his real motive."

Sam didn't respond to either the smile or her attempt at levity. His gaze was fixed on a Japanese lantern, but she could tell his thoughts were elsewhere.

Trina was on the verge of interrupting those thoughts when a steel-spined elderly woman did it for her. "Good morning, children," she enunciated, her keen brown eyes darting back and forth from Sam to Trina.

"Nice to see you again, Miz Lathrop," he said, the soul of politeness. "I trust you're enjoying your stay."

"I've not yet found cause for complaint. Be assured than when I do, you shall hear about it first, Samson."

If his parents had been looking for a biblical namesake, they couldn't have chosen better. "Samson? Your real name?"

"Only if someone's interested in testing my strength," he confirmed with a glare. "You game?"

She swallowed and shook her head, the image of his granite-like muscles still vivid in her mind's eye. "I'll pass."

Trina marveled at how the slightest allusion could rekindle her interest in Sam. That realization preyed on her until they were seated in the sunny, plant-filled coffee shop. Then their legs tangled under the table, and the ensuing vibrations gave her a new demon to contend with.

She must be a masochist, subjecting herself to a man who kept her so emotionally off balance and physically stimulated. It made no sense.

Just as it made no sense to consider his afterbreakfast invitation to look over his operation.

"I appreciate the offer." She did an exaggerated check of her watch, pretending dismay that it read ten. "I'd better get started if I'm going to make any time today."

"Look at it this way. There's a lot of miles between here and California. What's another few hours? I can give you a condensed version of the tour, then . . . we'll see."

She wavered, not because of any eagerness to leave, but because she couldn't comprehend Sam's reason for asking her to stay.

In spite of its shaky beginning their meal had turned out to be unexpectedly pleasant. He'd bombarded her with endless questions, mainly about her work experience. She'd done most of the talking, while he fed a large appetite.

He had paid close attention, rarely looking at anything except Trina. But his interest seemed more detached, almost businesslike, and that gave her confidence. She'd needed a respite from the constant sensual overload.

Now he wanted to further delay her departure so he could show her around. The Trina who had only recently begun taking risks couldn't say no. "A tour sounds great. Shouldn't I clear out of the room first so housekeeping can make it up?"

His hand flicked in dismissal. "I'll send word for them to bypass it. We're not booked to capacity, so it isn't as though someone's waiting to check in."

Trina dug for her wallet and signaled their waitress. Coffeepot at the ready, the young woman scurried over at once, mindful of serving her boss. "Please bring me the check. I'm treating."

A phantom grin almost broke the thin line of Sam's lips. "Becky," he said, rising, eyes on Trina, "Ms. Bartok's money is no good here. Isn't that right?"

"If you say so, Mr. Wonderful," Becky agreed without a second's hesitation.

Trina stood to minimize his advantage. "Does anybody around here ever disagree with you?"

"Not when they know I'm right." His impressive shoulders lifted slightly. "Given the circumstances, I am judged to be right a good part of the time. Things run smoother that way."

Trina conceded the point, though reluctantly. "My parents owned a restaurant. I have a natural aversion to walking checks and forgetting tips."

"You waited tables? What kind of restaurant?"

"Hungarian. But, no, Papa would never allow me to wait tables. He'd say, 'Use your brain, Trina, not your hands.' He made sure I spent most of my time studying."

On their way out she saw Sam slip something into Becky's pocket. "His advice must have paid off. You worked your way into a pretty decent job for someone so young."

Anton's advice had not been good or bad per se. It was just that by always accepting it without question, she had relinquished control of her own life and future. "The thing is, I really did want to wait tables and help Mama with the cooking, wanted to be in the middle of family activity instead of being banished to a corner with my books."

"In that case why don't we start our tour in the kitchen? Who knows, maybe we'll put you to work so you can satisfy your frustrated desire."

Their eyes met while his words echoed between them like a ticking time bomb. Frustrated desire. For perhaps the first time Trina understood the true meaning of the phrase.

Again she pondered the lunacy that kept her here when any sane woman would have been long gone. She'd awakened determined to get on with her dual quests of searching for her brother and finding a job. Instead, she had allowed Sam to deter her, and she wasn't sure why. Did she still harbor hope that he'd change his mind and offer her the assignment? Or worse, was she simply unable to pass up the chance to spend more time with him?

Telling herself that a quick tour couldn't distract her from her real mission, she said, "The kitchen it is. Mama always said that's where you find the heart and soul of a place."

Two hours later they hadn't made it beyond the facilities in the lodge's main building. Kitchen, laundry, health club, hair salon, theater, or bowling alley, wherever they visited, Sam introduced employees and encouraged them to talk about their jobs. It amazed her that he knew each of their names, as well as a staggering amount of trivia about their personal lives.

She also noticed that not one of them presumed the same familiarity with Sam's private life. She stored that in her memory bank. "How do you keep track of all these people and details?"

The question seemed to puzzle him. "Nothing hard about it. If I don't know the person well enough to be sure he'll do the job my way, he doesn't get hired in the first place. Keeps things simple and minimizes turnover."

He might not dress or talk like the career-driven types she'd encountered in the past, but Trina could see that Sam Wonder took care of business on his own terms.

They exited from the lower level, and he put on a pair of sunglasses. One look and Trina's heartbeat did a stutter-step. Wearing those shades with faded jeans, boots, and a starched white shirt, he struck the perfect balance of cowboy and cool. He even had the walk down pat, a loose-hipped stride that looked as if he'd just dismounted. That she found the total package so devastatingly attractive was her misfortune.

A short distance away he stopped by a poolside

snack bar. "Let's grab some fruit and cookies. That ought to hold us while we cover the rest of the grounds. Then we'll get lunch."

The man was seldom without something to eat in his hand. He had cadged samples the entire time they were in the kitchen, and that was immediately after feasting on a huge breakfast. "Is food all you think about?" she asked as he bit into an apple.

He paused midcrunch. At first the grin was visible only in his eyes. When he lowered the fruit, it enveloped his whole face. "I think the term is sublimation, isn't it?"

Touché. Bring it up, get your nose rubbed in it, she scolded herself as she took a vicious chomp of her own apple.

Sam commandeered a golf cart from a maintenance worker and steered them down the twisting road to the marina at the foot of the hill. "One phase of the expansion will include more docking slips for visitors who come to eat or gas up."

Trina estimated existing spaces for about fifty boats; half were occupied. "I assume visitor load is heavy enough to justify the cost." The remark sounded presumptuous, as if her input mattered.

"Take a look at the lake today. Two weeks from now, you won't recognize this as the same place. The water will be churning when the season gets in full swing."

"Memorial Day is the unofficial opening, right?"

"Right. We always throw a barbecue to kick it off. It's been a tradition since early on. We're kind of superstitious about it. A big crowd for the cookout is supposed to be the forerunner of a successful season."

For a brief moment Trina looked ahead to the event. Sam and his crew of enthusiastic employees would no doubt pull out all the stops to guarantee a fun time. But she squelched the errant longing to be part of it. Two weeks might as well be an eternity. "I wish you hordes of hungry barbecue hounds and your best year ever."

He toasted her with an oatmeal-raisin cookie. "Here's hoping." They rounded a curve, and he stopped to point at a narrow cove. "We're going to tuck a second marina in there. It will be reserved for guests who bring their own boats, as well as for the lodge's rentals."

"You mean like the one you used to get home last night?" She had lain awake several hours, thinking of Sam navigating those deep, dark waters by himself. She'd even fancied that he might share her loneliness.

"I didn't have to borrow a boat after all. I went by to pick up something in my office and ran into a friend as he was leaving the nightclub. He offered to drop me off."

"Oh." Of course he wasn't lonely. Why should he be?

"Matt insisted. Truth is, I'd rather have taken the shortcut. That time of night the water is still and as smooth as glass. The quiet is all yours."

From what she'd seen, he thrived on people and the activity surrounding him. Beneath that, could he be a loner at heart?

"Ever take a boat out by yourself, Trina, when it's so dark and cloudy not even the moon can show you the way? Push it hard and fast with no destination except another state of mind that feels better than the one you're in?"

"No. I haven't had much experience. With boats." Then again, they weren't talking about boats at all. He knew. *He knew!* Understood that restless yearning for something so elusive it defied words.

"At times I— Aw, forget it." Sam glowered at her as if she were to blame for his fleeting brush with self-revelation. Then they began a slow climb back up the hill.

Neither said anything for long, torturous minutes. When he finally did, he sounded like a tour guide once more. "Over there by the basketball court we're going to add badminton, shuffleboard, volleyball, and horseshoes. Most places I've checked out are limited to golf, tennis, and swimming, plus a few pieces of exercise equipment they advertise as a health club."

"Whereas Chimera aims to offer something for everyone?"

His index finger massaged the slight hollow in his chin. "We try to cover all the bases. Give 'em good food, superior service, their choice of nonstop activities, and they'll have every reason to come back."

It was a straightforward concept of serving customers, one too frequently forgotten. "Apparently the formula is working if you need to add more rooms."

"Speaking of that, we'll be trying something new this time. Individual cottages that allow more privacy." He veered off the pavement onto a path that cut through the woods. "They'll be built here, among the trees."

For the next few hours Trina fell victim to Sam's excitement. Time slipped by unnoticed, and concern about her own future vanished. She was too involved with asking questions, offering suggestions, and picturing how Chimera would look once the improvements had been made.

He was seducing her on yet another level, and he wasn't even trying. Trina found herself tempted by illusions of security and permanence, the very things she'd cast aside.

They traded the cart for his Bronco, then drove to the golf course and ate lunch overlooking land where preliminary clearing had begun for another nine holes.

Last stop was the sprawling greenhouse and gardens complex. She learned that much of the produce, flowers, and fruit used by the lodge was grown on the property.

Riding back, Trina reviewed the day's itinerary and all she had learned. Chimera was a thriving little empire; Mr. Wonderful the hub around which it rotated. She couldn't help being impressed. She also couldn't help feeling envious. Unlike her, Sam knew exactly where he wanted to be and what he wanted to do. He belonged.

He parked the Bronco alongside her Porsche. Although he switched off the engine, he didn't let go of the keys. "Looks like I've monopolized your whole day."

A whole day. She had been here almost twenty-four hours, most of them spent with Sam. Now she'd run out of excuses to stay longer. "I enjoyed it."

"And what did you think? Your overall opinion of the place and my plans."

"I think you've done an excellent job of creating a vacation paradise, and that your additions will make the resort even better and more prosperous."

He nodded, still inspecting the keys. "What would you say to staying on, helping me out with the financial end?"

Her universe tilted slightly; she clutched the door handle. "You're kidding!"

Sam faced her, green eyes glittering with intent. "Make no mistake, Kat-a-rina, this project is very important to me. It means . . . everything. I don't treat any part of it lightly."

"No, I'm sure you don't. It's just that I can't understand why you're asking me to work with you."

"You said it yourself, you're qualified. This morning I talked to Dad. He called you a genius with figures."

Trina rolled her eyes. "I'm afraid 'genius' overstates my talent considerably. Besides, after the way Robert schemed to throw us together, why would you trust his word on anything, especially me?"

"I asked would he recommend your work if you were sixty years old, snaggle-toothed, and cantankerous."

She didn't know whether to laugh or be offended. A chuckle won out. "I can't wait to hear what he said."

Sam was stingy with his smiles. When he gave in to one, it was worth the wait. "I think his exact words were, 'Son, I'd still have to recommend her work. But my conscience would trouble me a lot more than it does today.'"

"Sounds like he's unrepentant, even knowing that we've caught on to his mischief."

"Dad repent? He's too busy feeling smug because things worked out just as he wanted. He got you here, and I've asked you to stay."

Trina stiffened at the resentment shading his voice. "It's obvious you're not completely sold on the idea. Why bother to make the offer?"

"Damned if I know."

She didn't believe that for a minute. "It doesn't strike me as a good enough reason for either of us to alter our plans." She began gathering up her purse and bag. "Thanks for everything, but I can't accept a job just because you want to make amends for Robert's interference."

His lips flattened in a thin line. "Forget Dad. This business is between us now. I want you to stay."

Why the sudden about-face? What was behind Sam's offer, and did she dare consider it? "I need some time to think."

She saw rather than heard him sigh. "Fair enough. Take an hour or so. By then it'll be dinnertime. We can check out the Friday night seafood buffet, and you can ask all the questions I'm sure you'll have."

Trine knew she couldn't leave without exploring this business between them. "Where shall we meet?"

"The lobby. At seven."

"All right. I'll see you there." She hopped out of the Bronco before either of them had second thoughts.

Alone in her room, Trina collapsed on the still-unmade bed. Sam was right about one thing. She had plenty of questions. Possibilities and problems warred with one another inside her head.

A job here would justify putting California on temporary hold. Back when she'd been committed to change, she had declared her new life would be free of deadlines and timetables. So far she hadn't adapted very well to the lack of structure. Remaining in the Ozarks would be a chance to test her resourcefulness and flexibility.

Besides, after a month she truly missed the challenge of work, and, ego aside, she was convinced she could do justice to this project.

However, Chimera was synonymous with Sam Wonder. She'd spent the day with him and could tell he'd be a hands-on executive.

"I can feel those hands now— Oh, holy Hannah!" she exclaimed, leaping off the bed, thoroughly disgusted with the suggestive image that appeared in her mind. And therein lay the primary drawback of being around Sam for even a short time. Given the slightest provocation, her erotic fantasies took center stage, full blown and in living color. Trina could not perform effectively until she did away with that obstacle.

She told herself she needed to shower because she felt gritty from a day outdoors, but she set the water temperature several degrees cooler than normal. It felt wonderfully soothing on her feverish skin.

She also told herself that she was a woman in control of her thoughts, actions, and emotions.

Exerting the same control over her more primitive instincts would eliminate the problem.

By the time she entered the lobby to meet Sam, she had her armor in place. Too bad she hadn't hung on to at least one suit. She could have used a more tangible form of armor to bolster her resolve.

The reception area was large and open, resembling the great hall of a British manor house. An alcove to the left held registration and the cashier. On the right was a room furnished like a parlor, with wing chairs, camelback sofas, bookshelves, and a fireplace.

She spied Sam sprawling over the better part of one sofa, munching bar snacks as he read a magazine on hotel management. As soon as he saw her, he put aside the magazine and stood. "Thought you'd never get here. I'm starved. How about you?"

Food was the least of her worries. "Sam, is there someplace we could go for a few minutes? I'd like to speak to you in private."

He crossed his arms and closed one eye, as if weighing whether it would be worth it to insist on dinner first. "I guess we can go to my office."

He ushered her down a corridor and through an almost-invisible door that led to a suite of small offices. They all looked neat and functional, though far from plush. She silently approved. Well managed companies spent money on their products and services, not on luxurious surroundings for executives.

Sam's office seemed to be the same size as the rest, a detail she found rather endearing, since its square footage was inversely correlated to his importance. He motioned her to take the one extra chair. "What's so hush-hush that we have to discuss it in private?"

Trina smoothed the collar of her coral linen shirtwaist, wishing she could command as much authority as he did in his uniform of jeans, white shirt, and boots. Every time she saw him, he appeared to have changed into a fresh outfit, but it was always identical to the one before.

Sam dropped into the big chair, swiveled it to the side, and propped his chin on his palm. The pose showed his profile in much too favorable a light. Trina found herself wanting to trace the smooth plane of his jawline. It always looked as if he'd just scraped it with a scalpel. "It can't be things like job description, fees, benefits, term of employment, the usual interview stuff."

"True. All that can wait."

His hand dropped and he turned to face her, watchful. "What is it that *can't* wait?"

"I'd like to accept your offer. There's only one condition. If you're serious about us working together, you must agree to it. Otherwise, I'm gone."

"And that is?"

Trina tried to disguise the deep breaths she was taking to calm her seething stomach. "This thing between us, this . . . chemistry, or however you choose to define it . . ."

"Yes?" His voice was as wire-tight as hers.

"As of right now . . ."

He surged from the chair, dominant, commanding, and all male. "Yes, Trina, as of right now, what about this *chemistry*?"

"It has to end."

Three

Sam felt his mouth drop open at the same time as he dropped back into his seat. Of all the conditions Trina might have imposed, this was the least expected. It astounded him that she had chosen to deal with the issue head-on after they'd taken such pains to dance around it.

Maybe her way was best. Get it out in the open and get rid of it. He could testify that ignoring the attraction hadn't lessened it. If anything, he felt the pull more strongly after spending the day with her. Introducing Trina to his world, sharing his dreams—because that's what the plans were a result of—had somehow deepened the connection.

And increased the danger tenfold.

"Surely you're not going to deny it exists."

Hearing her speak again roused Sam from his stupefied silence. He risked a glance at her. Sitting there in her prim little dress, hands folded in her lap, she looked a whole lot calmer than he felt.

"Well, no. Wouldn't be much point in denying it."

"Which is why I want your assurance that the only reason you asked me to stay is you want me to do the job."

He rearranged two stacks of papers on his desk while mentally arranging his words. "Bottom line is I need advice from someone with your expertise. You happen to be here, so common sense says you're the logical choice."

"Maybe. But that doesn't preclude, pardon the cliché, mixing business with pleasure."

Sam took heart when he saw her hands start pleating her skirt. It made a guy downright nervous to deal with a cool-as-a-Popsicle woman when his gut was bumping and grinding like a carnival stripper. "You're referring to a certain kind of man who'd push, take advantage in this kind of situation."

"But you're not one of those." She seemed very eager to establish his honor.

"No, I'm not one of those." Truth. Sam had never pushed or taken advantage of a woman in his life.

She fixed her gorgeous eyes on him. They weren't a perfect match in shape. The left lid was the slightest bit sleepy. It drove him crazy. "Does that mean we have a deal?"

Deal? He struggled to recall what they were negotiating. Ah, yes. Mending their ways. "Since we're laying our cards on the table, I might as well tell you I'm relieved you don't want to get involved in anything hot and heavy."

Her eyes widened a moment, then her lashes veiled them. Pink tinged her cheeks. "No, an involvement would be reckless and irresponsible."

Sam felt both. For a few seconds he was tempted to vault over the desk and grab her. Ten years of caution kept him glued to his seat. "My life suits me fine as it is. I'm not looking for a woman or anything else to change it." Half truth. He *was* looking for some kind of change; he just didn't know how to define it.

"Oh," she breathed, sounding as relieved as he'd claimed to be. "I'm so glad to hear you say that, Sam, because I really think I can do an outstanding job for you. I already have some ideas based on our tour today."

"Good. I'd like to hear them first thing Monday morning. I try to set aside weekends for play." He saw a flicker of uncertainty in her eyes. "Relax, Trina. No more chemistry, remember?" The dreaded word.

"Yes, of course." She went back to work on the skirt, lining up damp pleats. Sam's blood heated when he envisioned those soft, smooth hands working on him. "It shouldn't be hard."

"Not hard at all," he said hoarsely. Lie. Talking about what they *weren't* going to do was making him want to do it more than ever. He rotated his chair to the side. It didn't ease the pressure. "We're adults, not libidinous teenagers."

"Who can't control their natural urges," she added, angling her body toward his, unconsciously, he was sure.

Was that a shadow of cleavage just above the top button? He meshed his fingers and rested them in his lap. "You know, we'll probably laugh about this once the job's complete." Now, however, Sam was not amused.

He was obsessed. What hung from the end of that fragile gold chain framing the neckline of her blouse? Had it absorbed the warmth of her breasts, the scent of perfume?

"I'm sure you're right. We'll have a good laugh." Her smile was hardly more than a nervous twitch of her lips.

Sam realized he hadn't been very subtle. His eyes had followed the path of his thoughts, and his tongue . . . *Damn, Wonder! Get a grip.* Trina wasn't interested in a quick tumble, and neither was he. In a few weeks she would be gone, and he'd be here. Alone again. By choice, he reminded himself.

"See how easily we came to a consensus?" He'd agree to anything to get out of here before he did something uncivilized. "Shows we'll make a great team." He urged her toward the door. "How about that seafood I promised?"

"I've been on an eating orgy ever since I got here. At this rate I'll be as big as a cow by the time I leave."

"That I can't imagine." Trina was reed-slender, and he figured it had little to do with dieting. "Call it a working dinner. We still have to hammer out a few details."

Sam switched off the light and cupped her elbow, bent on proving he could play the chivalrous escort. But the lightest contact, even in the guise of manners, rekindled the fire. His fingers flexed, an involuntary caress. All the talking, all the agreeing, hadn't meant diddly.

He wanted her.

• • •

Trina pirouetted before the full-length mirror in her spacious new room, one of the perks of her job. Like everything else today, the calf-skimming fuchsia palazzo pants buoyed her spirits. She tugged on a coordinating tunic length T-shirt with broad stripes of fuchsia, teal, lime, yellow, and orange.

She smiled at her brightly clad reflection. This was the image she'd always wanted. "Robert Wonder, you old fox, I might have to thank you after all."

His meddling had given her a necessary reprieve so that when she resumed her journey it would be with a clearer sense of purpose. A few weeks here meant nothing weighed against fifteen years.

In all that time thoughts of a reunion with her brother had consumed her. Beyond that she hadn't thought about how to actually find him. Nor had she ever considered failure, which now emerged as a distinct possibility. Taking to the road had forced her to face reality.

Tracing Tony was still her top priority, and she intended to persevere. His parting words came back to her. "I think I'll head out West, Trina. Maybe I'll find my place there." And maybe she would find hers there too.

The secret dread welled up within her again, bringing with it a knife-edged pain she'd grown used to. She could still hear her father's cutting voice repeating that Tony wanted nothing more to do with his family, especially her. It had almost become easy to believe. After all, they had remained in the same place as always. He knew where to find them if he'd cared enough to try.

Yet Trina had never given up completely. When she'd graduated from college and got her first job, she hired a detective to find her brother. After months with no success the man concluded that Tony had taken steps to make sure no one could track him down. How she'd hated to admit that perhaps Anton had been right all along.

At that point she'd locked away her feelings, and not until after she received a substantial settlement from her father's insurance policy did she consider another search. Something inside her wouldn't give up hope. She had to try once more.

In the meantime she had a project to focus on, and nothing could diminish her upbeat mood. Come Monday, she'd begin solving a problem, and she was eager to tackle it. Until then she aimed to spend the weekend wallowing in self-indulgence.

After pampering herself with a room-service breakfast, another perk, she'd gotten a pedicure and splurged on several sporty outfits from one of the arcade shops. Sam had told her to forget dressing up city-style, that casual attire was the norm for employees who didn't wear uniforms. No secret where that decree originated.

Sam. Trina's exuberance for the job was tempered by a nagging worry that she'd overplayed her hand with the dramatic scene in his office. She had thought by confronting temptation she could neutralize it.

Unfortunately Sam looked every bit as appealing across the desk or the dinner table as he had the first time she saw him.

"I'll deal with that tomorrow," she hedged, stowing her valuables in a canvas tote bag bearing the Chimera logo. "Right now, the *Ozark Belle* awaits."

She slipped on a pair of new boating shoes and took off for the marina.

Trina joined the line to board the riverboat replica, anticipating old-time elegance along with some lake lore and legend. This was probably the only time she'd visit the area. Might as well see everything while she was here.

A blur streaking across the lake caught her attention. At this point it was nothing but speed and motion. Still, Trina watched. The blur became a boat, coming in fast, seemingly on a collision course with her.

Her warning system kicked in. Sam Wonder.

At the last second he whipped into a tight turn, churning up a rooster tail as he circled; then he repositioned the boat and cut off the engines. It slid into a berth as if magnetized.

Trina suspected he'd been showing off. Men who looked like Sam frequently did, and invariably got away with it because the world was full of impressionable women. "Join the club," she grumbled, miffed that she was one of them.

She knew nothing about boats—not that they came in so many colors . . . or that they could be sexy. Sam's, navy with gold pinstripes, rode low in the water, looking sleek and fast as a greyhound, and he piloted it with the flair she aspired to when she drove the Porsche. Had the boat been a car, it would have been a racer. "Not bad, as entrances go."

He lifted his shades and dropped them, barely enough time to give her a view of green eyes lightened by the intense sun. "Looks like I made mine just in the nick of time. Hop in."

"What about my tour?" The *Belle*'s whistle

sounded its final call to passengers. "This narrated cruise is supposed to be full of lake lore and local color."

His hand choked the throttle. "Yeah, but my cruise will take you a lot farther than Captain Kelly's. And I can fill you with local color until you beg me to stop."

Trina went hot all over. At the same time goose bumps dappled her flesh. Nothing had changed. Words and good intentions were worthless against Sam's potent magic.

So why didn't she keep her place in line rather than accepting his hand and hopping in? Was she addicted to living dangerously? If so, she'd come to the right place.

In retrospect she could see that yesterday's tour of Chimera had been more a test than a spontaneous show of hospitality. Sam had done it to assess her reaction to the place. Her enthusiastic questions and comments, her approval, had led to the job offer.

Something told her his motivation for this boat trip was entirely different. She was also afraid it wouldn't stand up to close scrutiny.

He started the engine, letting it idle while Trina stowed her bag under the foredeck. Then he backed from the slip and very sedately guided the boat to the mouth of the cove. Once they hit open water, he turned to her and said, "Hang on." He shoved the throttle all the way forward, and the boat's bow lifted out of the water. In a matter of seconds they were skimming along the lake's surface at warp speed, and she sat back, exhilarated.

Over the din of the powerful inboard motor, Sam

pointed out mile markers, and they hadn't passed many before he docked at a busy lakeside restaurant that obviously catered to boaters. "Lunchtime."

"What about my tour?" she demanded as they climbed steep steps up to the patio.

With a touch to her elbow he steered her to a table. "Plenty of time left for that. Surely you don't expect me to work on an empty stomach."

"As much as you eat, how can your stomach ever be empty?" She accepted a menu from the waitress who'd scurried over and greeted Sam by name.

"That's the point. Eat often enough and you don't take the chance that you'll ever go hungry." He waved away a menu. "They make great frog legs here, if you're interested."

"No, I don't usually eat that much at lunch. I'll take the chicken salad and fruit," she told their waitress.

Sam ordered the frog legs, plus an appetizer, extra salad, and blueberry pie for dessert. While they waited, he waved to several people at neighboring tables and spoke to more who passed by theirs.

"Do you know everyone on the lake?"

He shrugged. "I guess I know most everybody from around here. It may seem spread out, but this is quite a bit like a small town. And I've been here a long time."

"Ten years, you said." Trina squeezed lemon into her iced tea.

"That's how long since I moved here. But I've been coming all my life. From the time I was six years old, I spent most of every summer here with my grandparents. I never wanted to go back to St. Louis when it was time for school to start."

"So you always wanted to live here?"

"Always. I got sidetracked in the city for a while, but it turned out okay in the end." He moved his water glass, making patterns on the tabletop. "I probably needed the lessons I learned there. They gave me even more motivation to move here and succeed."

To start over, as he'd phrased it. Again, Trina was curious. "Were your grandparents in the resort business?"

"No, Grandad made some money in the postwar construction boom. He bought quite a few acres here when the land wasn't valued very high. It's heavily wooded, and the soil is rocky, so it's never been good for much besides logging and pasture for cattle."

"Is the lodge built on his property?"

"Yeah, and I wish he and Grandma had been able to see it." He paused, deep in thought. "I inherited all their land, but the lodge only used up a small amount of it. I kept plenty to make sure my house will never be crowded by neighbors."

"So having the land is what influenced you to start Chimera?"

He picked up a spicy buffalo wing from the just-delivered platter. "No, I'd always dreamed of something like Chimera. Having the land made it easier to pitch the idea to investors, and, naturally, Dad was instrumental in lining up the money initially. I could never have gotten started without his help and connections."

He sounded less than happy about having to

rely on Robert's assistance. Still, it had enabled him to get what he wanted. "It must be wonderful to see a dream come true, to live it every day." Trina hoped that day would come for her too. And she hoped it would be soon.

"When I had to think up a name for the corporation, I picked Wonderful! as a play on my name. But it's turned out to be a pretty apt descriptive word. I've been lucky."

Luck often came from working hard to attain one's dreams, and she suspected Sam had worked harder than most. While she had yet to prove her own ability to capture a dream, she had at least made a start.

Sam polished off the appetizer as his main course arrived, a huge platter of frog legs, potatoes, and vegetables. "By the way, I like that outfit you're wearing. Think I saw one like it in Sherri's."

She was amazed that any man would pay attention to the stock in a woman's specialty shop. But nothing should surprise her when it came to Sam's interest in Chimera. "Does even the tiniest detail escape your notice?"

"Not if I can help it. When you have a business, Trina, you can either turn it over to others and hope for the best, or you can take care of your own quality control, be a constant presence. I," he said, fingering the ribbed neckline of her shirt, "am the hands-on type."

In more ways than one, it seemed. She wanted to tell herself he was just evaluating the merchandise. If that were the case, why did his hand leave a heated imprint where it hovered? And why did she want him to keep touching when she'd been the one to forbid it? Trina grabbed her fork and attacked the chicken salad.

Later, after a second piece of pie, Sam pronounced himself fortified enough to press on. Trina planned to pay attention to the markers and keep track of the miles, but the streamlined boat covered them so quickly, she lost count.

They passed under a bridge, and Sam leaned over to say they would be entering the Grand Glaize arm of the lake. The significance of that eluded her, but she smiled and nodded interestedly.

Once they turned into a narrower channel, he slowed and steered close to an orange-and-white buoy. "This is Lake of the Ozarks State Park, and we're going to follow the aquatic trail. I'm not as good-looking or funny as the *Belle*'s captain, and I don't have a routine, but I can give you the high points of what we'll see."

"Give me your best."

What he gave her was a look hot enough to bond her to the boat seat. "Count on it."

She crossed her legs and leaned forward, an attempt to ease a sudden pang of desire that stole her breath. Though being around Sam always spawned a certain tension, Trina craved it. In addition to being devoid of risk-taking, her old life had also lacked zest. He supplied plenty of both.

At last he pointed to the top of a bluff where she spotted an unusual rock formation with a window clear through it. "What you see is a slice arch. The topography here is riddled with sinks, caves, underground streams, springs, and natural bridges. That's because limestone and dolomite are no match for the forces of water."

"You sound like a geology major."

"Given my choice, that's exactly what I might have been. Instead, I let someone else make the choice for me, and I ended up in business school." His ironic smile came and went quickly. "I try to think of that deviation as a blessing in disguise. Hard to run a corporation with a geology degree."

Trina had difficulty imagining Sam Wonder letting anybody make decisions for him. Granted, he'd been younger then, and probably more tractable. But who had exerted that much influence?

At every stop on the tour Sam delivered a folksy lecture. "I remember getting an 'A' in geology," she said, "but my retention of what I learned is zero. It makes so much more sense seeing examples in nature instead of reading about them in textbooks."

"Stick with me, Trina. I'll show you lots."

She didn't doubt him a bit. And most of it would probably land her in trouble.

They spent nearly two hours in the park before Sam announced it was time to start thinking about dinner. "We can stop by the lodge and pick up something to cook out and everything to go along with it." He grazed her cheekbones and the bridge of her nose with the side of his thumb. "Why don't you grab a bathing suit while I do that? You look like you could stand a dip to cool off."

Trina was sure her pinkness resulted from a combination of sun exposure and nearness to Sam. No way could she stay cool with him close. "I bought a new suit today at Sherri's." But did she dare wear it in front of him? It was hard enough not getting ideas with both of them clothed. Perhaps she ought to hide out in her room.

But when the time came, she collected her suit simply because she couldn't bear for the day to end.

They didn't go for a swim after all; Sam was anxious to get the marinated halibut steaks on the grill. Too relieved to argue, Trina put the rest of their meal together, and they ate on the deck as the sun reddened the western horizon above the tree line. Then they watched a video of a newly released action thriller.

"How about that dip now?" Sam asked while the tape rewound.

The idea of diving in the lake in the dark gave Trina the willies. She was more of a pool person. "I don't trust going in water that I can't see the bottom of."

He walked to the entertainment center and shut off the VCR. "I was thinking of the hot tub, not the lake. That's more my speed this time of night."

"You mean the one at the lodge?"

"No, the one on my deck. Outside my bedroom."

Just what she needed. Sam, his bedroom, and a hot tub. Talk about trouble. "It's been a long day. Maybe I'd better get back."

He pulled her off the couch. "Come on, Trina. I'll do you— It'll do you good."

That's what she was afraid of. But as usual she didn't protest long and loudly enough, and she ended up changing in the master bathroom. Which increased her anxiety level by quantum leaps.

When she slid open the door to the upper deck, Sam was nowhere in sight. Good. She could be submerged in the water before he saw her.

The deck was dim, its only illumination indirect, from tiki torches placed behind large potted hibiscus and plumeria. She paused to let the fragrant tropical atmosphere envelop her, lure her with the promise of forbidden treasures and stolen pleasures.

"Oh, stop romanticizing and fantasizing, Trina. He didn't invite you for that." Her fertile imagination refused to cooperate. How many women had Sam brought here? Seduced here? "Forget that too."

Trina dropped her towel on the deck and eased into the water. She leaned back, closed her eyes, and gave herself over to the swirling, massaging warmth. She was just beginning to relax when a shadow stole across her lids.

Her eyes popped open, but she had to immediately look aside. Sam Wonder in jeans was a work of art. In frayed cutoffs he sent her nervous system into meltdown. She tried really hard not to stare. Nature undermined her.

Why this sudden interest in muscles when iron pumpers had always left her cold? If men had to work so hard to advertise it, they must not be very secure in their masculinity. Sam wore his like a second skin, no advertising needed. Maybe the appeal lay in knowing his muscles came from physical labor, not health-club machines.

"Water feel okay?"

"Hot!" she blurted out, more accurately describing her internal temperature than the water's. "Uh, just right."

He knelt to tinker with the controls and timer, giving her a chance to study him unnoticed. She decided narrow hips and a lean torso were the perfect complement to his well-developed arms, shoulders, and chest. She could stare endlessly at the prominent tendons in his hands and forearms. The few freckles dotting his shoulders were almost as fascinating as the pattern of hair on his chest.

When he sat and dangled his legs over the edge, the water eddying around Trina got hotter. Arms stiff, he began to lower himself slowly. Dry-mouthed, she watched his eyes drift closed, his lips part, his tongue touch his upper lip. Then he plunged in fully.

Trina's body felt invaded. The breath she'd been holding flowed out with a rush. Her knees came together in a tuck that only increased the ache. All of this and he hadn't even come close to her.

Sam heard Trina moan. His eyes snapped open. She looked flushed, but he didn't see any way she could be as overheated as he was. She had spread her arms on the apron, lifting her upper body out of the water. What was visible was way too much, and not nearly enough.

Talk about something mundane, he ordered himself. "So what do you think?"

She looked straight into his eyes. "It's better than anything I've ever seen before."

Sam managed to keep from groaning aloud. He could *not* keep from looking at her breasts. The white bathing suit concealed little. Not shape or size or the shadowed thrust of her nipples. Damn! He'd known bringing her here was a mistake, but he'd insisted on it anyway.

He inhaled and tried to get the conversation going again. "How would you like to go waterskiing tomorrow?"

She was doing her best to look at anything besides him. "I've never tried it."

"I can . . . teach you." Why couldn't he just leave her alone? Sniffing around Trina like a hungry hound ranked right up there with his all-time stupid moves. The kind of moves that cost a man more than money.

"I'm not very . . . athletic."

She confessed it as if it were an intimate secret. Sam wanted to probe until he found something really intimate. "I promise I can get you up."

"Get me—"

"Up. On skis. I'm strong."

"I know."

Oh, hell. He hadn't meant to draw her attention to his chest. Those clear, penetrating eyes had a way of prodding him to say rash things. "You ever been married, Trina?"

It was an innocuous enough question, but he had no reason to ask it. And no reason it should get him hard. Make that harder. Just looking at her had given him a head start.

"No," she said a little sadly. "I guess I never believed I'd still be alone by the time I reached thirty. But the years got away from me, and it happened."

Sam forced both hands behind him, holding one with the other. He didn't think he had ever wanted to touch a woman as badly as he wanted to touch Trina at that moment. The only thing stopping him was the certainty that if he did, he wouldn't let go for a long, long time. By then it would be too late. For both of them.

"You know," he said, straining to sound philosophical, "I think there are times when, no matter how hard we try, fate steps in and we lose control of our lives."

Her hand covered her mouth; he thought he could see her lips quivering before she submerged it again. "There are times when I wonder if I ever *had* control of mine."

He shook his head once. "A beautiful, sophisticated New York City woman with doubts? Doesn't add up."

"Being born and growing up in New York doesn't make us immune to the same insecurities everyone else has."

It was then that he realized what he wanted most. It wasn't her body, though he was near to desperation for that too. But he had to find out what drove her west when she didn't have a set destination. And why it was imperative to him that she stay.

She looked frightened, as if he'd spoken his intentions aloud. "It must be past midnight. I ought to go."

Sam allowed her to climb out of the hot tub, to put a safe distance between them. "Trina?" He swallowed hard when she turned back around, looking wary but expectant.

She raised one hand defensively. "Sam, I'm sure this is not a good idea."

He pushed himself out of the spa and closed the distance between them. "It's madness, and we both know it."

She grasped his wrist as he reached to touch her face. "Then why are you giving in to it?"

"Because, Trina, I don't see any help for it."

Four

He was right. There wasn't any help for it.

Trina touched the hammering pulse at the base of her throat, so strong she knew he could see it. She heard its echoing drumbeat inside her head. Sam's mouth hovered so close, she felt its moist warmth teasing her lips. She fought to keep her eyes open but gave up, hypnotized by the compelling need that radiated from him.

"I'm going to kiss you, Trina."

"Yes."

"You're not going to stop me."

"No. I can't." She'd gone beyond wanting to, probably was past being able to.

One of his hands shaped the back of her head, fingers tangling in her hair. He anchored the other at her waist. Then his mouth covered hers. The way he kissed reaffirmed what she'd already learned about him. He was a man who knew what he wanted, and he took the most direct route to get it.

Here in the moonlit stillness, she curved her arms around his neck and granted him the right to claim as much as he would.

The melding of their tongues was like slow dancing to sexy music—two bodies in erotic alignment, swaying in the languorous motion of seduction, acting out a heated emulation of lovemaking. The taste of him, the sleek wetness of the inside of his mouth, made her dizzy, made her want . . .

Her hands clamped to his waist, kneading, digging into the hard flesh there, nails raking his skin as she sought more. He groaned, and the rush of pleasure dazzled Trina, pushing her beyond the boundaries of a first kiss.

That was alarming enough in itself. Even more so was the realization that she didn't want to stop. Which was why she had to stop now.

"Ohhh," she said, expelling a breathy, mournful sigh. She peeled herself away from him, scooping up the towel she had dropped when Sam reached for her. "I guess it was inevitable that we'd have to test what that would be like." She rubbed her lips. It was akin to pressing the taste of him deeper. "But now that we know, we have to go back to our original plan."

His pent-up breath came out with a whistle. "That's going to present kind of a problem."

Trina refused to ask why, mainly because she half suspected what his answer would be. It would match her own.

"See, I liked holding you, tasting you. I want to do it again. Right now. And often."

She threw up one hand, though he'd made no

move toward her. "But, Sam, you gave your word this wouldn't happen."

"I don't think so. Seems to me I agreed it *shouldn't*. No way could I guarantee it wouldn't. There's a difference." He engulfed her protesting hand in his. "Trina, if at any stage of that kiss you'd shown me you weren't with me all the way, it would have been over. Don't forget that it did stop as soon as *you* gave the sign."

Trina hung her head, chastened. "You're right on all counts." There'd been no force, not even the slightest pressure. She couldn't hold him accountable when she had gloried in his hunger, encouraged it.

Turning away, she wrapped the towel around her waist. "I know I must sound like a broken record, but we have to fight this, not let it control us. Otherwise, we'll end up with a disaster on our hands."

He said nothing, just allowed the silence to expand until she couldn't endure it any longer and faced him again. Then he said, "'Disaster' is a trifle melodramatic."

"Label it anything you choose. The fact remains that I have never had a vacation fling in my life and am not about to start now."

"You aren't on vacation," he pointed out with a hint of mockery. "The reason you're here is to work."

"Thank you for refreshing my memory." Trina had counted on Sam to be more receptive. But she knew it was unrealistic to expect too much cooperation from a sexually frustrated male. He'd held her close enough and long enough to brand her with the passionate demand of his body.

Though she shared the blame for his condition, she saw no point in belaboring it. And from now on, she would assume full responsibility for seeing that tonight's scene wasn't repeated.

"You've shown me a very interesting time today, but I'd better get back to my room. Besides, I think everything's been said."

"At least until Monday," he added, a reminder that no matter where she went or what she did, Sam wouldn't be far away.

"Where do you want to start?"

Trina had known she'd be working closely with Sam. She hadn't figured that meant a temporary desk in his small office. Maybe she'd get lucky, and he would spend the majority of his working hours in the field. "I'd like to review your financial statements first."

He swiveled his chair around to the credenza behind him and pulled out a drawer. "How far back do you want to go?"

"All the way to the beginning. I want to get a fix on assets and liabilities over the entire ten-year period. After that, I'll need to see details and numbers for the two previous expansion projects."

Sam plucked out an assortment of bound reports and carried them to her desk. "Copy whatever you need, then return these to my file." He dropped a key ring on top of the stack. "An extra set of keys to this office, my desk, and the files. There will be times you'll need stuff, and I won't be here. In fact, I'm on my way to meet the architect. It's all yours."

As soon as the door had closed, Trina murmured, "I guess that solves the problem of proximity for a while."

She picked up the first financial statement without opening it. It occurred to her that Sam was uncommonly trusting to allow a stranger access to his private documents. But she supposed contracting her for this position implied a high degree of trust. Had he relied solely on Robert's judgment or his own gut instinct?

Something told her that when the chips were down, he would go with his intuition. Whether it involved long-range planning for the company or handling employees, his unique management style would send most MBAs scrambling to a textbook for black-and-white evidence of why it wouldn't work. Except that it did work, for Sam.

Trina's business instincts weren't that finely honed. She preferred to make decisions based on facts gathered from research and detailed computer analyses.

Did that mean their contrasting methods would clash, making it impossible for them to work together? "Dimwit," she jeered, flipping to the first page. "We won't *be* working together, not in any real sense."

She would gather her data, make the appropriate recommendations, then get out of the picture and leave the decision-making to Sam. "This isn't a partnership, Trina."

In the following days she had to remind herself frequently of the limited role she played in the grand scheme. But it was hard to remain detached and objective when Sam went out of his way to involve her in his plans. Each new facet deepened her fascination with Chimera, and by extension, its owner. She was hooked.

Mornings he usually left Trina to her figures. Around noon most days he was back, insisting she accompany him on a scouting trip on site. Her horizons expanded hourly. He taught her the basics of well drilling, surveying, rock blasting, and road paving. She offered suggestions about decor, furnishings, and amenities for the new guest accommodations.

By the second week, workers had got over their curiosity at seeing Sam and Trina together. Everyone must have assumed that they had a strictly business relationship, an impression Sam went out of his way to foster.

When they were alone, he spent most of his time looking at her like a man who was interested in a woman for all the obvious reasons. But he didn't touch. Not once.

Trina wavered between gratitude for his restraint and irritation . . . for the same reason. She burned with the remembrance of his kiss, the strength of that long, firm body pressed against hers. In the darkest part of the night, she ached to feel it again, that sweet madness.

Memorial Day madness. The whole place was caught up in it. At one end of the patio an eight-piece country band tuned guitars and banjos and did a sound check. A portable smoker had been puffing away since early morning, causing mouths for miles around to water. The chuck wagon, complete with gingham-shirted attendants, stood ready to serve roasted corn, ranch-style beans, coleslaw, watermelon, and countless other goodies to accompany the barbecue.

Everyone connected with the lodge was dressed in western wear. Even Trina had succumbed. She looked down at her jeans, chambray shirt, and vest, all trimmed with tapestry inserts.

"I'm not sure this contemporary cowgirl look is me," she confided to Paige, Sam's cousin who had arrived earlier that day.

"Trust me, with your build any old rag you want to throw on is your look." Paige stuck out her tongue, but her malice was playful. "Us short girls spend our teens hoping we'll grow up and have legs all the way to there, like you."

"Guess we're never satisfied," Trina said. "Tall girls slouch around feeling gangly and awkward. We dream of being petite and graceful and bubbly, like you."

Paige rolled her eyes. "Look at it this way—you get all the tall guys, and they fit you so much better."

Trina let that pass without comment, though it brought back powerful memories of how snugly she had fit with one particular tall man. Her gaze strayed to the opposite side of the patio, where it linked with Sam's just long enough to speed up the cadence of her breathing.

Paige maneuvered her away from the crowd. "Now tell all. What's with you and Sam?"

"I beg your pardon?"

"Sweetie, when my cousin has been seen daily

in the company of the same woman, it's news." She struck a pose. "Especially when that woman looks like she's fresh off a fashion-magazine cover and speaks with an exiled-princess accent."

Trina sank onto a picnic bench. Did people here really see her that way? As some glamorous foreigner? Talk about farfetched. "I'm a temporary employee, no more. In a few weeks I'll be gone. I thought everyone understood."

Paige dissolved into giggles. "Uh-huh. I suppose you think Sam makes a practice of chauffeuring all his employees around. Or sharing with them the details of this new development he's planning."

Paige was bubbly, all right, a bubbly buttinsky. "Everything you mentioned comes within the framework of my job." Most of it, anyway. "I work for the man. It's unavoidable that we spend a certain amount of time together."

"Granted. What about the cozy dinners and boat trips on weekends?" Paige picked Sam out of the growing throng and sent him a cheery wave. "Are you telling me you talk about business then?"

"Yes, we do." She defied Paige to argue. When she didn't, Trina relented. "Sometimes."

"Okay. Then that leaves us with nothing to go on but the way he watches you. Like he's watching you now."

Trina made one last stab at denial. "You're going to have to do something to curb that lively imagination."

"Hey, I know my cousin. And I've never seen him with that I-can-give-you-what-you-need look in his eyes for any woman. Not even that witch Marianne." She slapped her thigh. "Hot damn!

After all these years, the old boy's sap is flowing again. Don't you just love it!"

Trina felt her blaze as red as Paige's bandanna. She opened her mouth to protest the crude innuendo, to clarify her relationship with Sam once and for all. But the specter of someone named Marianne choked her into silence. Who was she, and what did she mean to Sam? Worse, would she show up today?

"Hello, Cousin. I see you're playing the gadfly, as usual."

Trina started when she heard Sam's voice behind her. Thankful for the diversion, she glanced over her shoulder. "Paige and I were just getting acquainted."

"I suppose she was making a pest of herself." He challenged Paige with a boxer's stance. "Are you ready for another summer in the combat zone?"

"You bet. I've had nine months' practice." She explained to Trina, "I'm a phys-ed teacher in real life, but every summer Sam coerces me into spending my vacation as one of the lodge's recreation directors. We organize all sorts of fun activities. You'll have to come play with us."

Trina doubted that her idea of fun would correspond with a phys-ed teacher's. "Work keeps me pretty tied up."

"Oh, right," Paige said with a sly smile. "Well, try to set aside a little time for extra curricular too. Got to take our pleasures where we can find them." She made a fist, slapped it into her palm twice, and socked Sam in the belly. He barely registered the blow. "Ta-ta." She wiggled her fingers and slid into the crowd.

"Did I miss something, or does she go around punching everyone?"

"Paige is very competitive, prides herself on being harder and tougher than everybody else. She works with weights and runs ten miles five days a week."

"But she's so small."

"Yeah. She has this theory that men always take advantage of a soft woman."

Her stomach fluttered. That he had kept his hands to himself for two weeks was little consolation. There were other ways to touch. A lingering look, a secret smile at unexpected times. A longing gaze at her hands as if he wanted her to do something with them. The silent promises of his sensual mouth. The way his voice drew out "soft woman." Like a caress.

He set one booted foot beside her on the bench; his forearm stretched along his thigh, close to her shoulder. "Seems to me just the opposite is true. Any man worth the name values softness and will do his best to protect it."

Trina felt herself melting, telling herself all the while that it was ridiculous. "Your old-fashioned attitude would probably offend most feminists."

"All old-fashioned attitudes aren't necessarily bad. That's a lesson a lot of feminists still have to learn. Not every issue is worth a battle."

"I agree." Trina didn't want to battle over any issue at the moment. She could smell his soap and, as always, his heat. Sam's scent set off a taut internal achiness that struck her as vaguely animalistic.

"Here you two are," a jovial voice boomed. "Paige steered us in the right direction."

"I'm afraid the busybodies have descended in force," Sam muttered under his breath. "Hello, Dad. Mom. Glad you could make it."

Trina did a double take at the sight of Robert wearing denim. She'd never seen him in anything but banker's blue. Without his standard uniform he could pass for the prototype of Sam, though he was several inches shorter.

"Wouldn't miss it, son. Especially this year." He eyed Trina pointedly and smiled.

She stood and extended a hand, determined to play her role. "Robert, thank you again for recommending me for this job. It's been—" How to describe it? "Enlightening." In more ways than one. "Mrs. Wonder, it's nice to see you again."

"Call me Natalie, dear. After all, you're part of the family now." There were a few seconds of silence, then she recovered beautifully. "The Chimera family. Sam claims each employee is like a close relation."

Trina picked up the cue. "I've researched a lot of companies for clients. Few of them inspire the kind of enthusiasm and loyalty that Wonderful! does." She was starting to sound like another Sam Wonder groupie.

"We're very proud of what Sam's accomplished here. I think my parents would have been pleased at how effectively he's used their land."

"Okay, Mom, enough cheerleading," he said, taking her arm and pointing her toward the gazebo. "Monte and the band are about ready to begin playing. Don't you want to go say hello first?"

Natalie winked at Trina. "This is your chance to lower the boom on Robert. Don't hold back. I certainly said my piece when I found out he'd sent you here under false pretenses. Why, I was positively incensed, and told him so."

Watching mother and son depart, Robert chuckled, showing no sign of remorse. "That she did. My ears still carry the blisters." He cupped Trina's elbow. "Let's stroll while you take your turn at me. But be gentle, in deference to my advanced age."

Trina couldn't contain a laugh. Robert looked much too fit and active for that ploy to work. She imagined Sam would age equally well. "I've known you quite a while now. You've always been direct and businesslike. Why did I never suspect this devious streak?"

"The truth is, I seldom resort to such tactics. And I swear I didn't have this in mind when I invited you to visit us in St. Louis. It just clicked after I talked with Sam about the financing, then you showed up a couple of days later." There was an unmistakable twinkle in his eyes. "Nothing wrong in killing two birds with one stone, right?"

"It's a wonderful place to work, no play on words intended. But I'm afraid you've struck out in the matchmaking department."

The twinkle got brighter. "Admit it. You like him."

"Robert, you're incorrigible. Of course I *like* him. Everyone likes Sam. It's just that there's no possibility for a romance between us." How many times would she have to repeat this? "Before long, I'll resume my trip, so the geography is wrong. Besides, neither of us is interested."

"Geography," he scoffed, "is not a hindrance

when you want something badly enough. As for the other, I plain don't buy that garbage about neither of you being interested. Hell, I'm not too old to recognize the signs."

Could their attraction be so tangible, others picked up on it? That wasn't a subject she wanted to raise with Sam's father, so she changed it. "The smell of meat smoking has had my taste buds standing at attention all day. I think I'm ready to sample some."

"Suits me. Bet you can't wait to try our renowned Ozark specialty, barbecued coon."

"C-coon!" she sputtered. "I've never—"

"Never say never, Trina. About anything."

All afternoon and into the early evening Sam circulated, playing host. He shook hands or exchanged hugs with old friends, introduced himself to first-timers, and accepted compliments on another successful celebration.

The original idea for a cookout had been his, and each year he looked forward to continuing and expanding the tradition. It was symbolic, proof that dreams can come true, in spite of the naysayers.

In the past he'd enjoyed the gathering, but this year he felt suffocated by too many people. He was anxious for the festivities to be over so he could . . . what? All he really wanted was to carry Trina off someplace where they could be alone. He'd wanted to do that a lot lately, and the need kept mounting. It made him restless and testy. He had been that way a lot lately too.

"Trina seems to be enjoying herself," Robert

observed. "She was a real good sport about tasting the coon. Even went so far as to say it wasn't bad. I call that tactful."

Sam sought her in the crowd, something he'd caught himself doing every few minutes all day. He couldn't stop. "Probably the novelty effect. I'm sure her typical entertainment leans more to the highbrow."

"Could be. But give her credit, she's game. Heard her tell Matt she'd never square-danced, but that didn't stop her from trying. They cut a mean rug on the dance floor, in case you missed it."

He hadn't. "Stop needling me, Dad," Sam said, struggling to keep his voice even. "Don't bug Trina about it either."

Robert took a sip of his beer, savoring it like fine wine. "Relax, Son. What's got you so touchy?" He chuckled, a maddeningly self-satisfied sound. "You have my word I will never again interfere in your love life."

"I don't have a love life!" Sam bellowed. A few anonymous giggles nearby made him realize he'd shouted. "Well, damn!" As he stalked off, he could have sworn he heard another infuriating chuckle. Meddling old reprobate.

Sam had chugged a quart of iced tea in an attempt to cool himself down when the burst of gunfire came from a short distance away. Hoofbeats thundered. Men shouted. More gunshots rang out.

Here and there screams rose from the crowd, but guests familiar with the routine applauded and reassured the uninitiated that this was part of the show.

Two black-clad "outlaws" exploded around the bend, spurring their mounts to outrun the posse, a trio of a good guys dressed in white. The Wild West shoot-out was another gimmick they'd tried a few seasons back. Privately Sam considered it contrived and hokey, but the customers ate it up, so they'd retained the chase as a regular feature.

Matt, astride a stallion as dark as he was, taunted his pursuers into another round of gunfire. The spectators alternately clapped and encouraged or booed and hissed.

After a great deal of noise, dust, smoke, and yelling, the outlaws were subdued, captured, and marched away with their hands tied behind their backs.

Sam tried to spot Trina in the melee, but he couldn't locate her anywhere. He plunged into the mass of people, elbowing his way through. Twenty minutes later he hadn't caught up with her, and he didn't much like the way his gut constricted at the thought of her leaving without him.

"Looking for someone?"

Matt had discarded his black hat and horse but still looked very much like the desperado he had portrayed. He carried a longneck bottle, which Sam knew was mainly for effect. Like himself, Matt rarely touched alcohol. They both knew that booze and lake water could be a deadly mix. "Just casing the crowd."

"Uh-huh. Me too." Matt studied the label on his bottle. "Bunch of us going to the Silverado later. Play a few songs, dance a little. Want to come along?"

"No. Soon as I can work my way to the marina,

I'm out of here." As with plenty of other nights Sam had no plans other than enjoying his solitude. "I've had my crowd quota for the day."

"Yeah, go ahead and run off to your hideout. Me, I plan to look up Trina. See if she's in the mood to party."

Sam stewed in silence. Why had everyone picked today to goad him? Matt was the closest thing he had to a brother; they'd been friends since childhood. Right this minute he felt like slugging his old pal. He jammed his hands into his pockets, in case he was further tempted.

"That is one tasty-looking woman. Man would be crazy to pass up a chance at someone like her. Think I'll try my luck."

"Do, and I'll rearrange your face along with the rest of your moving parts."

Matt guffawed. "So that's the way it is. I figured as much. But I gotta ask, why are you standing around threatening me when you could be making contact with her? I'd wager that would give you a lot more satisfaction than doing damage to my ugly mug."

"Trina and I have a noncontact agreement." One he was having the devil of a time abiding by. Sam wouldn't lay odds on how much longer his "honor" could sustain him.

"Well, buddy, it's like those slick-talking lawyers tell you, contracts are made to be broken." Matt slapped Sam on the back. "Guess I'll go off in search of alternate companionship for the evening."

"Paige is here." Sam knew the barb was a spiteful retaliation, but he couldn't resist a payback.

Matt's expression turned arctic. "If both of us are real lucky, we can get through the summer without running into each other. I'll damn sure go out of my way to avoid that sharp-tongued shrew."

The long-term feud between his cousin and his best friend baffled Sam. Neither would speak the other's name, nor would they reveal the cause of their hostility. It was just a fact of life.

Like his craving to be with Trina. "Hell and damnation," he muttered, striking out for the wooded trail that wound around to the opposite side of the cove. "I can't go on this way, and it's time I told her so."

He found her in the small meditation garden deep in the woods, off the path. "This spot isn't described anywhere in the literature, or shown on any of the maps."

Just as he'd known where to find her, she didn't appear surprised by his appearance. "Not long after I decided to stay, I stumbled onto it by accident. I've been coming here ever since. The tranquil setting makes me reflective."

"Which is what its designer intended. He pitched it to me something like, 'This should exist as a reward for those wise enough to listen to themselves.'"

"What a lovely sentiment."

"Shobi isn't sentimental, though he does have quite a bit of the mystic in him. What the heck, the guy's done a fantastic job. He says we need this, I say do it."

Trina swiveled on the stone bench and gazed up at the darkening sky. She had changed into shorts, and Sam made a valiant effort not to stare at her legs. "It's official now. Another successful opening under your belt, another season in full swing."

He dropped onto the other end of the bench. He'd put in an endless, hot, exhausting day, and coming here was not going to give him any relief. "Did you have a good time?"

She treated him to a little smile. "It was nice. Overwhelming, but nice."

"Nice is a generic word, one you use in place of a real compliment. If you found it silly and boring, say so. I don't bruise easily."

"I didn't mean that at all. I felt so . . ." She waved her hand in a gesture of confusion. "Oh, don't pay any attention to me. I'm in the throes of a self-pity attack. That's why I sneaked away."

Sam leaned forward, bracing both elbows on his knees, hands loosely clasped between them. "What brought it on? This attack of self-pity?"

"A combination of things, I guess. All the camaraderie here, especially today, the sense of belonging that everyone takes for granted. It just emphasizes that I'm an outsider."

"Did someone say or do anything to make you feel that way?" He'd have that person's head before the night was over.

"No, of course not. Everyone goes out of their way to be friendly and helpful."

"They'd better. We built our reputation on friendly service." Her laugh sounded dry, forced. Sam knew right away he'd said the wrong thing.

"Yes, you have the stars and diamonds and rave reviews in all the guides to prove it works." She surged to her feet. "And like every other guest, I'm temporary."

There was a missing link, but Sam was too irritable for subtleties. "You're in a strange mood, Trina. Why don't you come right out and say what's bugging you?"

She stared through the trees in the direction of the lake. "You've made a place for yourself, obviously doing something you care about."

"You had a place in New York, from all accounts a good one. Yet you chose to walk away from it. Why?"

"It was never *my* place. I simply ended up there by following my father's orders. Now I want to make my own. But I got cold feet en route, which is why I latched on to your job opportunity. Today made me see that was a mistake. I should have kept going. I can't put it off any longer."

"You told me you have nothing definite in mind for California. Why all of a sudden is it mandatory that you rush out there?"

"So I don't get cold feet again."

The desolation in her tone disturbed him, made him want to hold her. He stood and grasped one of her shoulders, bringing her around to face him. "Let's hear the rest of it, the *real* reason you're so upset."

Her shoulders slumped; one hand massaged the other. "My brother disappeared fifteen years ago. I haven't seen or heard from him in all that time. It's tormented me like a wound that won't heal. Now he's the only family I have left, and I can't get on with my life until I find him."

The stark confession staggered Sam. All along

he'd pictured her as a pampered sophisticate. The reality she painted was quite different. "You mean there's nobody anywhere? No relatives at all?"

"Maybe a few scattered ones in Hungary, none that I know. My parents fled Budapest just ahead of the Russian tanks. Since they would never go back, even for a visit, they lost track of everyone. You must see why it's crucial for me to find Tony."

"I can appreciate the need for a family connection, sure. As for putting the rest of your life on hold while you trace your brother, it makes no sense."

She drew back as if he'd struck her, but her voice was deadly calm. "Easy for you to say. You're not alone in the world. You didn't lose a brother, someone you loved and idolized. You haven't spent years haunted by the fear that it was your fault he left."

Sam reached for her, but she backed away. He could see her trembling. "Trina, you're overreacting. What I was getting at is that you can't build a future based on someone else and *his* expectations. Go after what *you* want."

"All I want is to find Tony. And I'm leaving first thing in the morning to do it."

The night air shimmered, warm and close, almost tropical. Sam broke out in a cold sweat. He couldn't let her go, not yet. But could he risk making her stay? At this stage he had nothing to lose. Deliberately keeping his voice cool and blunt, he said, "You're forgetting one small detail."

"What?" she whispered.

"You signed a contract. Don't even think about breaking it."

Five

Trina shook her head, an attempt to silence the ringing in her ears. Surely she'd misunderstood. Sam wouldn't make threats. "What do you mean?"

"I mean to forget taking off tomorrow. I'm holding you to the terms of our contract. Until you deliver, you're stuck."

She had run the gamut of feelings today—expectation, melancholy, resentment, and now anger. By far, outrage was the most energizing. "You can't keep me here if I don't want to stay. That's against the law."

His features were indistinct, but she could make out his exaggerated shrug. "So sue me. I believe signing your name on a contract is binding. A matter of honor, if you will."

"And I believe it's a matter of honor to see that my brother gets half of my father's insurance money. He's earned it."

Sam swiped his hand over his forehead and

through his hair. "If you're hell-bent on doing this, at least let me put you in touch with somebody who'll handle it right. You have to watch some of these fly-by-night characters."

"You know a detective?"

"A private investigator in St. Louis. She specializes in missing persons. If Tony can be traced, Sara's a good bet to do it. And if she doesn't think you stand a chance, she'll level with you instead of taking your money and coming up empty."

Trina had learned about that scam firsthand. A few years ago a New York detective had strung her along for months before giving up. She'd felt discouraged and used.

"Thank you for offering to help. And you're right, a contract is an obligation. I won't leave until I've done the job." She might as well be waiting here while the investigator initiated the search.

"Good." Sam's extended hand was both a courtesy and a peace offering. "Now come with me. I want to show you the grand finale."

Trina supposed she should refuse, but knowing her time with Sam was finite heightened her need to make the most of what was left. "You mean there's more?"

"Uh-huh. My favorite part."

They took a roundabout way to the marina, avoiding the crowds. After Sam handed her into the boat, they cruised out into the main channel of the lake. He turned the boat back toward the lodge and anchored, leaving only the running lights on. "It's almost time."

Just then, the first explosion shot upward, a pulsing golden sunburst bordered with fountains of red. "Oh!" Trina exclaimed. "This is fabulous! One of my first memories is of Mama and Papa taking Tony and me to the Battery for the Fourth of July. I was maybe five, and I'd never seen anything so beautiful as all those colors in the sky."

"Let's move to the back seats where we won't have to look through the windshield. There's more leg room, and I have drinks in the cooler."

After they made the switch, Trina delved into the cooler and found a container of the snack bar's fresh-squeezed limeade. She poured each of them a glass and settled back to enjoy the show.

Sam emptied his glass and held it out for a refill. "Every season we try to add a new feature to the program so repeaters will have some surprises too. We started the fireworks about five years ago.

Trina's earlier lethargy vanished. "Know what I think would be spectacular?"

Sam grumbled something under his breath before saying, "No, tell me."

She plunked her plastic glass into one of the drink wells. Her hands made an encompassing gesture. "Boats are synonymous with the lake. There are thousands here at any given time. Why not sponsor an after-dark regatta?"

His glass joined hers. "Okay, I see the picture. What's the angle?"

Trina respected anyone who could cut straight to the heart of a matter. Sam did it better than most. "It's a contest, as well as a parade. Each boat is decorated with lights—that's the only requirement or restriction.

"The lodge can underwrite it, but you'd also

want to get merchants and businesses into the act. Pick a panel of judges, award prizes, play up the competition. It'd catch on, don't you think?"

With only the green and red running lights for illumination, she couldn't read his expression. "You may have something. Seems to me a lot of those folks flash their boats as extensions of themselves. Watch me. See how fast and powerful I am."

"You mean like this bullet we're sitting in right now? I haven't seen anything that comes close to flaunting male dominance more overtly."

She heard him hiss and uncoil from the relaxed, leg-extended slouch. "Are we getting Freudian here?"

"No! Not at all."

His index finger drew a line from wrist to shoulder, leaving behind a trail of sparks. "Trina, I have this boat because I like the water, and I like speed."

"I understand."

A thumb slipped over her collar to massage her sensitive nape, the motion slow and delicate. "And if I want to make a statement of my masculinity, I take the direct route."

Trina sat motionless, waiting.

"Like this." He was so quick and so strong that she found herself draped across his legs before she had time to object. Then his mouth claimed hers, and she forgot why she'd want to.

Light engulfed her. Brilliant splashes of color erupted overhead, all around them, filling the sky. She closed her eyes to everything but Sam, and the brilliance of her inner vision was just as dazzling.

His lips were hard, demanding. They allowed her no retreat, no hesitation, nothing but complete involvement. Once he was assured of that, they gentled, became playful, coaxing. He bit, with just enough force to make it exciting, and invited her to return the favor. He licked. Trina's tongue met and joined the moist stroking, conveying her pleasure with tiny moans of acquiescence.

His mouth deserted hers, leaving her breathless and needy. But, oh, the heated dampness as it trailed over her cheek left her trembling. "You have luscious lips, Trina. Know that?"

Her head moved from side to side because she couldn't speak.

"That first night, at my house, you licked them. I wanted to do it too. I hated wanting it, especially so fast, and I fought it."

His breath grazed her ear like a warm mist. "I know," she murmured plaintively, wondering if she would be able to continue her own fight. The security of his embrace was so tempting.

"But these . . ." He lifted the hand that she had curled around his biceps and brought it to his mouth. "These are what drive me out of my mind." His parted lips skimmed lightly over the top of her hand before turning it to leave a wet, lingering kiss in her palm. "They're so soft." He gave equal time to the other hand.

"My mother made me use lotion constantly. So they wouldn't be like hers. Ahh!" Now he was moving them over his face, shaping all those sharp angles and delectable hollows she'd longed to explore. "Spending so much time in the kitchen at the restaurant made hers rough and red."

Stop babbling, Trina. But how else could she retain a grip on sanity, however tenuous? "Why do soft hands matter?"

She felt the vibration in his throat, a cross between a laugh and a groan. "You wouldn't ask if you could peek into my fantasies. Believe me, soft hands play a very prominent part in those."

"Sam," Trina protested, attempting to pull her hands away from his guided tour. The struggle ended with them fanned over his chest, spanning those world-class pecs. She whimpered. "We both know this will lead to big trouble."

"Honey, it already has." He shifted her, not that she needed further evidence of his claim. His arousal had been apparent from the instant he'd nestled her in his lap. "And as of tonight, there's no more fight left in me. I'm going to kiss you and touch you as often and as intimately as I can get by with. It's your call from now on."

His tongue delved inside her mouth fully and forcefully, and Trina was powerless to hold back the rush of sensation that greeted it. Heaven help her. Sam Wonder, no holds barred, was a force too elemental to deny.

She didn't mean to do it, but her arms locked behind his neck. She didn't plan to sink her fingers in his close-cropped hair, to twist and clench and tug the strands until he groaned and told her to keep it up. And she never intended to possess and devour his mouth as if he was the best thing she'd ever tasted, though he was.

He said something, but the words were muffled

by the depth and intensity of their kiss. Trina's head dropped back; they exchanged gasping breaths. She wished she could could see him, verify that his eyes were as glazed as hers, that his skin was as flushed. She knew he was as hot.

"Help me, Kat-a-rina. Lift so I can bring you closer."

She was too lost in passion to be of much assistance, but he had no problem turning her to face him. Now her knees framed his hips, forcing their bodies into provocative alignment. She wiggled her bottom, trying to keep from brushing against him too suggestively. He anchored her hips and moved to compensate, locking them together. "Now you can wiggle all you like."

"Anybody ever tell you that you have a wicked streak, Sam Wonder?"

"Wicked" was a good term to describe his laugh. Because she didn't hear it often, the sound of his laughter was like a special gift, just for her. "Uh-*uh*. I've always been told I'm a good . . . boy."

"I'll bet."

"You don't believe me?" He laughed again and sent Trina's pulse rate into the danger zone. His laughter also sent heat flowing to her most feminine depths, the part of her that knew Sam would be very, very good. The part of her that wanted to find out just how good.

"Oh, I believe you." She moved against him. The fit was perfect. It was as if she had found where she belonged.

He grunted and held her in place, kneading her outer thighs. His thumbs strayed beneath the hem of her baggy shorts, making arcs as they inched upward. He came so close to touching her where she desperately needed him to. "This time, you kiss me, Trina. Make it hot."

A seismograph could have picked up her internal tremors. If she kissed him now, she couldn't help but make it hot. She was burning. "I can't think, Sam."

"Good. This is not an intellectual exercise."

True. Her brain was barely functional, while the rest of her raced ahead at Mach 2. She wanted this one kiss to transcend the best he'd ever shared with another woman. Trina didn't stop to question why that was important. She just knew it was.

Reminiscent of the first time they had touched, the fusion of their lips seemed to sizzle, but the electricity didn't stop there. She sought his buttons at the same time he burrowed beneath her oversize T-shirt.

"Yes!" they exulted simultaneously, and her fingers gloried in the firmness of his chest while he made fast work of the front clasp of her bra.

His hands covered her breasts, squeezing gently. "Soft here too. I knew you would be." Then they glided over her sides and midriff and her back. "Soft everywhere."

Trina had been making her own discoveries, her fingers delighting in the breadth and firmness of his chest and shoulders. "I don't think you're soft anywhere."

"Times like this, honey, Nature didn't intend a man to be soft." His tongue bathed her ear. Trina shuddered and clung to him possessively.

"Oh, Sam . . . when you say . . . things like

that," she got out between labored gasps, "it makes me want—"

"I know. I want it too. Bad." He lifted her away from him and eased her into the seat beside him.

All her senses were alive, her body humming like a tuning fork. But her mind was confused. He wanted her badly, yet had called a halt.

"Trina, you need to think long and hard about whether you want to go where this is leading us. If you do, I'll take that as a sign you want more than a quick fling. I'm not the type to settle for a short-term involvement."

Trina felt raw and vulnerable, and she was torn. From the beginning desire had been so urgent that she'd half convinced herself she could handle an affair. Now Sam was saying that wasn't enough for him, which made the decision more complicated. "You've known all along I'll be leaving."

"All I *know* is that you can do whatever you want. The choice is yours." He got up and felt his way forward to the controls, tugging Trina by the hand. "So you decide where our next stop will be. My house or the lodge?"

She understood the question beneath the options. Going home with him would signify her acceptance of his terms. "To the lodge. I need time if I'm to think long and hard."

"All I can say is I hope you come up with the right answer, and soon. I can't survive many more nights like tonight." He fired up the engine. "Hold on tight. I'm going to give you a wild ride."

• • •

Trina glared at the budget figures in front of her. To her disgust, she couldn't make heads or tails of them. She would have put them aside gladly, except on this Monday that was turning out to be anything but typical, Sam had come in the office and had spent the entire morning at his desk.

He used the phone a couple of times, but didn't make much pretense of working. Mostly he just watched her; at least that's what she caught him doing every time she sneaked a peek. It was a very subtle form of intimidation.

Or was it seduction?

He must know her thoughts were dominated by what had happened between them in the boat Saturday night, and the ultimatum he'd issued afterward. She cursed his conditions and her own vacillation.

Trina tried to add some numbers from the various cost estimates, but quickly lost her concentration. The obvious solution was to keep their relationship professional. Then the strings he'd attached would become irrelevant. It wasn't as simple as it sounded.

There was also the issue they'd argued over after the barbecue. Sam didn't agree with her objective, yet he'd offered to supply the name of an investigator who might be able to help her.

If she contacted the woman in St. Louis right away, it would give them a head start. Maybe luck would be on their side and the detective would find her brother right away.

As the tension increased between Sam and her, the quest for Tony gave her something to focus on besides the vexing decision she faced. Trina set the papers aside and met his gaze across their desktops.

"You know that investigator you told me about? Sara, I think you said her name is."

"Umm, what about her?"

"If you'll give me her full name, I'd like to call her and get the ball rolling."

His face didn't register any emotion, but she thought his spine stiffened. "You're determined to pursue it?"

She cautioned herself to remain cool, and said with utter conviction, "Reuniting with Tony is the most important thing in my life."

His lips compressed to an almost invisible line. He crossed his arms and silently challenged her statement. But in the end he backed down. "She'll ask you a lot of questions before deciding if she'll take the case."

"I realize that. I'm prepared to give her all the help I can." She meant it, but the prospect of taking concrete steps scared her a little. So many things could go wrong.

He sighed and drummed his fingers on a stack of glossy promotional brochures. Sighed again. "It would probably be best if you talked to her in person. Let me call and see how soon we can schedule an appointment."

"Sam," Trina started to protest, but he had already begun dialing.

Ten minutes later he hung up and announced they had an appointment on Friday. "We'll leave right after breakfast and get there in time for an early lunch. Sara will see us at one."

Us. "Thank you for taking care of it, but I really don't expect you to go with me."

"I'm going. That's a fact."

He said it with such certainty, she didn't bother arguing. Secretly she was glad he'd insisted. She had a feeling she might need moral support.

Sam stared at the phone, deep in thought. "Trina, I hope you've considered the possibility that even if Sara takes you on, it doesn't automatically guarantee success. Fifteen years is a long time. A lot can happen."

She pounced on a pen to occupy her shaky hands. "You have no idea how often I've told myself the same thing you're saying. I'm optimistic, but I'm also a realist."

"Just as long as you're aware of how this may turn out . . . so you won't be too disappointed if . . ."

"I'm prepared, Sam, however it turns out." Brave words. She hoped she could back them up. But she ought to not dwell on worst-case scenarios before they even got started. "You must know Sara well." Over the phone he'd identified himself only as Sam, and Trina couldn't help overhearing the friendly and personal nature of their conversation.

"We met about ten years ago. I needed her expertise." He paused a beat, the challenge back. "To do some checking up on my wife. Sara's efforts helped me keep Marianne from getting her mercenary hands on a single acre of this lake property."

An attack of chills raced over Trina. Marianne, the witch. "Your w-wife?"

"Ex. For ten lucky years now."

If he'd set out to strike her dumb, he couldn't have done a better job.

"Don't look so stunned, Trina. There's a lot of it going around these days."

"I know, but I didn't— I thought—" Thought what? That'd he'd waited thirty-seven years until she came waltzing into his life? The idea was ludicrous, and she couldn't imagine why it popped into her head. "Never mind. It's none of my business."

He conceded that with a nod, then added, "Unless you care to make it your business. Unpleasant as it is, it's something we'll need to hash out sooner or later."

Her tongue felt swollen, her mouth dry. "Later," she croaked. It was naive and inappropriate to be upset that Sam had been married. As he'd pointed out, plenty of men had. She'd even dated a few who'd gone through a divorce, and it hadn't bothered her in the least. Why this time?

Because, a smug inner voice informed her, Sam Wonder is different from any other man you've known.

Desperate for a change of scene and lacking any other excuse, she grabbed her tote and jumped up. "Come on. I'll buy you lunch."

"Why, thank you, Ms. Bartok," he said, standing and giving her an exaggerated bow. "That's the best offer I've had all day."

She managed to steer clear of the topic of his marriage during their meal and for the rest of the week. Not until they were in the close confines of the Porsche driving to St. Louis on Friday did she give in to the morbid curiosity and ask to hear the whole story.

Sam's jaw clenched, and he didn't speak for a time. She wondered if he was deciding what to censor or simply trying to condense the story into a minimum of words.

"I met Marianne at the lake between our freshman and sophomore years of college. Her parents had just moved down here, and she hated it, wanted to get back to the city. That should have been a tip-off, but I was young and . . . smitten.

"The next year I changed majors. After graduation I took a corporate job, and we got married. Marianne was determined to be a high-powered career woman, and it annoyed her to start out in low-level management. She complained endlessly that the climb took too long. She wanted the big house, a status car, exclusive club, designer clothes, and all of it right now!"

He blew out a breath, then began again. "I went along with as much as I could because she would nag me until I did. Within two years she was singing a different tune. She wanted to be a wife and mother. Okay, I agreed because I'd always wanted a family, though I resented her changing the rules on me in the middle of the game. She quit her job to relieve stress so she could conceive. After six months with no results she announced we needed to get away—an expensive vacation, of course—hinting that I hadn't devoted the proper amount of time and energy to getting her pregnant."

It poured out of him now, like a flood going over a dam. "I couldn't quibble with that. Hell, what man wouldn't lose interest in sex when he's up to his eyeballs in debt trying to maintain the lifestyle she'd insisted on when we had two incomes.

"Things went downhill from there, and it wasn't long before Marianne demanded a divorce, saying she wanted freedom to find a man who cared about pleasing her. She didn't get any argument from me on that front. I'd already come to the conclusion that I could spend a lifetime and not figure out what she wanted, other than piles of money."

He glanced at Trina for the first time since he'd started describing his marriage. "I was a damned fool to fall for her in the first place, and I let her make an even bigger one of me before it was over. But it's been finished and done with for ten years. The time since has been good for me." He looked over at her again. "Any questions?"

"No questions," she replied softly. "I'm just sorry you were unhappy." His story hadn't made her want to leap with joy, but it helped her understand why he prized being in control. It also distracted her from the coming meeting.

She was going to sit down with a stranger and bare her soul about what she'd come to view as a family tragedy. Since her father had forbidden her and her mother to speak about Tony in any context, she'd never discussed her feelings and fears with anyone. Anxiety built with every passing mile.

Whether it undermined her new independence or not, she was glad Sam would be with her.

They stopped for lunch. Sam ate and Trina watched, her throat and chest too constricted to swallow food, though she wouldn't deprive him for anything.

"Try not to worry," he told her, squeezing her hand. "Sara's a sweetheart. You'll like her."

Sara had a small suite in a single-story building in a nondescript suburban office park. Trina didn't know what she'd been expecting, but this wasn't it. Nor did Sara fit the image she'd created for her.

Short, rounded, rosy-cheeked, and soft-spoken, Sara Lloyd looked like the quintessential grand-mother. "I know what you're thinking," she said after Sam introduced them and they had shaken hands. "Everybody does. They expect someone more imposing. P.I.'s are supposed to be either hard-boiled or wisecracking, like in fiction."

Trina studied her, warming to the older woman immediately. "But your appearance is a boon, isn't it? I imagine no one suspects the motives of a sweet-looking lady who might have just finished baking cookies."

"Bless your heart, you're right. The real me is as good as a disguise. You'd be surprised to hear what some people tell me without my even ask-ing." She led them over to a comfortable conver-sational grouping in a corner of her office. "Now let's have some tea and chat."

Watching Sara pour tea into dainty bone-china cups, Trina let go of part of her uncertainty. She felt instinctively that she could trust this woman.

Sara took a sip, then blotted her lips. "Now, dear, tell me something about this brother of yours, starting with his full name."

Trina drew a deep breath and began reciting the facts. "Anthony James Bartok." She gave the date and name of the Brooklyn hospital where he'd been born, then patted the bag beside her. "I found his birth certificate when I sorted through my parents' papers. I have it with me."

Sara nodded. "Chances are he requested a copy at some point. How many years did you say he's been gone?"

"Fifteen. He left a few months before his eighteenth birthday." Memories of that terrible day came rushing back—her father's and Tony's bitter shouts, her own terror that this time their argument might turn violent, the despair of Tony's parting words.

"He said, 'I think I'll head out West, Trina. Maybe I'll find my place there.'" Her teacup started to rattle against the saucer. She grasped it tighter to still it, but that made the clattering worse. Sam took the china from her, then covered her hands with one of his.

She gave him her silent thanks with a strained smile. "I begged him not to go. There was nowhere he *could* go, and he had nothing to run to. But he said there was no alternative. He just couldn't take it another day."

The three sat quietly for what seemed like minutes, reflecting. At last Sara asked, "Was Tony a victim of abuse?"

Trina gasped and clutched at Sam's hand, needing an anchor. "Abuse!" She analyzed the harsh word. "I never thought of it as such. Not in the physical sense, certainly."

"And yet, a seventeen-year-old boy felt he couldn't take it another day at home," Sara said, her voice gentle. "What drove him to that extreme?"

"Tony and my father were always in conflict. Always. They were both so strong-willed, determined things would be done their way. I guess it was inevitable they would clash."

"Let's explore another area. Was your brother a typical bad boy? A troublemaker? Misfit?" Sara might be a crackerjack investigator, but apparently she was also a counselor.

"He was popular, had lots of friends. He did get into minor scrapes at school and some petty incidents in the neighborhood. Nothing major, but enough that they always called Papa." She recalled the way Tony treated her, protecting and indulging her and accepting her adoration as his due. "No, Tony was never bad or mean."

"It sounds as if most of his difficulties stemmed from the father-son relationship."

Sara made it so easy to open up, to make connections she hadn't thought of before. "You have to understand Papa's motivation. He wanted so much for his children, wanted them to take advantage of all the opportunities America offered."

"Trina's parents fled Hungary right before the uprising," Sam explained to Sara.

"Yes, they escaped with only a few of their possessions. They refused to talk about it, but I'm sure of this much—it was an experience that neither ever forgot. It influenced everything they did for the rest of their lives."

"I can see how it would." Sara went to her desk and got a notepad. "Trina, I realize my questions may sound like part of a therapy session, rather than the prelude to an investigation. But I have a theory that tracking a person is sometimes easier if I understand his reasons for disappearing in the first place."

"Makes sense to me." Trina began to think positively about Sara's chances of locating Tony. She had a good feeling about the woman and her methods.

"Now, is it correct that your brother has not once attempted to contact any of the family since the day he left?"

"No, he hasn't." That was the part Trina had the most trouble understanding and accepting.

"And 'out West' is the only clue you have as to where he might have gone?"

"I've racked my brain for something more specific." She shook her head, staring at her fingers, which were entwined with Sam's. "But I always come up empty."

"Any idea what kind of work he'd choose?"

Trina's head snapped up. "Isn't it strange? In all the times I've thought about Tony, I only visualize us being together. I never picture him having a job or family of his own, though I'm sure he probably does."

"What about his interests? Anything particular he liked to do?"

She flashed back to an image of Tony when he was about ten. "He liked to build things. He had sets of blocks and logs and was always constructing houses with them."

"Anything else? Places he was drawn to?"

Another flashback, this one at the beach. "Water. He loved the ocean, to look at it, play in it."

Sara scribbled several things on her pad. "At the

time he left, what kinds of identification did he have? Driver's license, Social Security card, passport?"

"I'm sure he must have gotten a Social Security card—he had a couple of summer jobs—but no driver's license. Papa didn't think we had any reason to drive a car. And no passport. Americans had no business traveling outside their country."

Sara chewed the end of her pen and studied her few notes. "I'll level with you. We don't have much to go on here. If a person is determined to drop out of sight, there are a thousand ways he can accomplish it."

Trina's stomach plummeted. She looked to Sam for support, but her thoughts were too scattered to guess his.

"On the other hand," Sara continued, "the computer age has made the impossible doable. We can only try, and if that's what you want, I'll try my best."

"It's what I want."

Sam let out his breath.

Trina turned to him, apologizing with her eyes. "It's what I *have* to do."

Six

"You still think I'm making a mistake with this, don't you, Sam?" They had concluded the meeting with Sara and were headed for the interstate that would take them back to the lake. Trina had to admit second thoughts were beginning to plague her, and was thankful Sam was driving. She wouldn't have been able to keep her concentration on the road.

"I haven't changed my original opinion. It's logical for you to want to reestablish ties with Tony. Nobody can dispute that. But its unreasonable to stake your future on it. In the end don't count on anything except what you make for yourself. It's the only way to be happy."

Sam the loner. She'd suspected that beneath the surface of the garrulous businessman lay a solitary heart. In a way it was sad, because from all indications, he had been eager and trusting and unselfish before Marianne put him through an emotional wringer with her constantly changing demands.

Oh, he was still generous, though from a distance. He gave freely of what mattered least to him. When it came to feelings, he withdrew, becoming wary and observant.

"I have to disagree. I believe we ought to build our futures with others in mind. That's the kind of security I'm looking for, not money."

"Who said anything about money and security?"

For a second Trina wondered if she was overdoing the candor. "Papa drummed into us all our lives that money equals security. He even steered me into banking because banks control money." He just didn't trust them with what he'd saved. Thanks to his paranoia, Trina herself harbored a touch of the same distrust.

"Too many people see money as the solution to everything. And too many of them do unspeakable things to get their hands on it."

Another lesson courtesy of his ex-wife. "You have to understand how starting over later in life affected my father's thinking. In Hungary he worked very hard at a menial job. He didn't earn much or have much, but what little he'd accumulated had to be left behind when he escaped. That's why he was so adamant about his children not being forced to do physical labor. He pushed us to achieve so we would have job status and security. He thought it was a crime not to take advantage of all the opportunities America offered."

She leaned her head against the high-backed seat and closed her eyes. "He stayed in an Austrian refugee camp for a while. That's where he met my mother, who was all alone too. Then they were allowed to come to the States."

"That must have been overwhelming. What did they do?"

"First thing, they both got jobs in a restaurant. Papa was ambitious and a tireless worker. Eventually he got a chance to buy the restaurant."

"And did well with it, I'll wager."

"Oh, yes. Papa wasn't about to waste his chance to succeed. But the hours were brutal and the workload heavy. That's why he was fanatical about Tony and me excelling in school. He wanted us to get good jobs and save our money."

They were approaching the outskirts of the city, and Sam speeded up. "But Tony didn't buy that?"

"In retrospect I can see that it wasn't the principle he rebelled against, but the fact that Papa didn't permit him to make his own choices."

They were going quite fast now, and Sam shifted into fifth gear, the one she never used. He definitely had the elan to drive a Porsche. "Doesn't it strike you as ironic that while you were the good one who did exactly what she was supposed to, you're now rebelling just like Tony? Why?"

"I guess it finally dawned on me that I was nearly thirty years old, and if I was ever going to take charge of my life, I'd better not waste any more time."

"And taking charge meant starting over?"

"It's a little hard to explain." Especially to someone who had his life so together. Sam wouldn't understand her inability to articulate precisely what she was seeking, apart from Tony.

"I've talked about nothing but family problems all day. You must be sick of hearing them. To be truthful, it's starting to depress me. Let's switch to something fun. Your choice."

"You got it." He slid out of the passing lane and slowed the car. At the first exit ramp he got off.

"I should have known," Trina teased, eyeing the fast-food joints ahead. "Give the man his choice, and he'll jump at food every time."

Sam took his eye off the traffic just long enough to startle her with a fleeting, but bone-meltingly sexy grin. "Sure about that, are you?"

The temperature had soared, and Trina fiddled with her air-conditioner vents. She'd asked for a switch, and he'd given it to her fast. The trip so far had been devoid of the sexual energy that usually surrounded them. Now that it had reappeared so suddenly and powerfully, she felt as if she'd been struck by lightning.

He fooled her, bypassing the restaurants in favor of a U-turn under the highway. When she saw he intended to backtrack toward the city, she asked, "What in the world are you up to, Sam?"

"You said you wanted to switch to something fun. I aim to please." There was that momentary grin again. It could make a woman weak-kneed and numb-brained.

"Forgive me if I'm a little suspicious. The last time we set out on one of these adventures, I ended up chilled to the bone because my clothes got soaked and it was sixty-two degrees outside."

"Yeah, the scenery was great, wasn't it?"

Late one night Sam had insisted they stop for a quick pass through the water park. Trina's tank top had got wet, and her body was outlined in graphic detail. Sam had looked—boy, how he'd looked—and she could tell he was dying to touch. But they'd been in their hands-off phase then.

"You still haven't said why you reversed directions."

"We're going to spend the night in St. Louis."

He tossed it out matter-of-factly, but excitement coiled inside her. She told herself overnight didn't have to mean *together.* "We didn't come prepared. Where will we stay? What about clothes and . . . and everything else we need?"

"Details. We'll do some shopping later. First I'm going to show you several of the little-known and lesser-appreciated tourist attractions in my hometown."

"I would like to see the Arch," she admitted.

"Aw, everybody does that. Hardly anyone takes time for the Bowling Hall of Fame. And I gotta take you to Coral Courts. It's too tacky to miss."

Sam had his way, but Trina stood her ground, and he finally consented to join the rest of the tourists at the Arch. The park surrounding the massive stainless-steel span was crowded, though Trina found it difficult to concentrate on anything besides Sam. She couldn't put her finger on what had cause it, but all day he'd been different somehow, more open.

They checked out the exhibits, then he bought tickets for the ride to the top, and they joined the line. Trina glared at him when he kept urging people to go ahead of them. He just shrugged and smiled. That was another thing he'd been doing more often lately.

When they were the only ones remaining in line an attendant motioned them to board the tram. The tiny capsule could ferry five passengers in close quarters. They were alone, just the two of them, facing each other.

"You weren't being nice to those people at all," she accused. "You were just—"

"Looking out for my own interests. There's a lot of me. When my legs tangle with somebody else's, I like to pick whose they are."

The erotic images his words invoked had Trina squirming in her hard plastic seat. "Behave yourself." She meant to scold, but ended up grinning.

"Just telling it like it is." His downward glance invited her to contradict him. Sure enough, one of his legs had snaked between hers. The other hugged her calf, just tightly enough so that she felt the warmth and the pressure.

He had her trapped, but the only frightening aspect of captivity was the anticipation it produced. "Does it take long to get there?"

Heavy-lidded, his green eyes pinned her. "You the kind who likes to reach the top in a hurry?"

Another erotic image, this one more detailed, suffused her with heat, filled her with an aching heaviness. Only Sam could inspire it. Only he could relieve it. But she couldn't think about that here and now, or she might be tempted to lunge at him and act out her lustful daydreams. "Please."

"I told you, I aim to. Wherever, whenever, and as often as you'll let me."

Her mouth and lips were as dry as ten miles of dusty road. Her tongue darted out to moisten them.

The low rumble in his throat was so primal, she'd have backed up if possible. "Lean forward, Trina. I want to—"

"Stop right there." She pressed one palm over her heart, which was galloping wildly. "It's crazy."

"That's what you make me, Kat-a-rina—crazy. Do you know how many times I've gone up in this Arch before today? Let me tell you, it's been so many I lost count long ago. Do you know how many times I've fantasized about being inside a woman while I was doing it? Not once."

"Oh!" This time it was not a visual image but a tactile one that left her reeling. She could feel the overwhelming, invading power of him and, in a rush of insight, knew that the decision about how far she would go with this man had been reached days ago. Perhaps at their first meeting.

Sam caught her hand and slowly brought it to the same position over his heart. Its irregular beat matched hers. "I want you closer, Trina. I want you, period."

His hand slid from hers, up her arm, and tugged. He nearly had her in his lap when the capsule bumped to a halt and its automatic door slid open. Their groans mingled as he helped her stand.

"Stay close, dammit," he grunted as they exited the capsule. "At least until I recover."

Trina stayed close the entire time they spent admiring the view from the top of the Arch, not to protect his modesty, but because she needed his nearness for a much more basic reason. If she didn't watch herself, she could grow dependent on having him nearby.

After leaving the Arch, they stopped downtown

for a shopping spree. Trina wasn't accustomed to spontaneous acts like overnighting on a whim or dashing through stores grabbing anything that caught her eye. Hers were not practical selections that she might wear often in the future. They were impulse buys, strictly for the moment.

When she met Sam at the designated time and place, he squinted at the overflowing shopping bags she held in each hand. "Looks like you bought enough for a week instead of one night."

"Look who's talking." He carried his own full shopping bag and a zippered bag from a men's store. Trina eyed her purchases ruefully. "They say it's a mistake to buy without thinking. But what the heck, it was fun for a change."

"That's what this is all about." He inclined his head toward an exit. "Come on. Time to go to the hotel."

He had said she'd find the hotel interesting; that was an understatement. She thought it was magnificent. The lobby, located in the Grand Hall of the renovated Union Station, featured a gold-trimmed ceiling, stained-glass windows, and gaslights.

To reach their rooms, they had to ride an old-fashioned brass elevator. "This used to be called the Headhouse," Sam explained. "When railroad crews had to lay over, they spent the night here. A new section with more rooms was added when the station was redone, but this part is original."

"As I was driving west, I tried to stay in Victorian bed-and-breakfasts or old hotels, if possible. Much as I like the benefits of the modern age, I enjoy stepping back into the past too."

"You'll get the best of both here."

Once the bellhop had situated them in their adjoining antique-furnished rooms, Sam rapped on the connecting door. When she opened it, she saw that his shirt was partially unbuttoned and he was barefooted. "Will an hour give you enough time?" he asked. "I thought we'd have a drink here and maybe walk along the river before we go to dinner."

"Sounds lovely. I'll see you in an hour, then," Trina agreed, feeling as though she were preparing for a real date with an incredibly desirable man whom she very much wanted to impress.

Telling herself she ought to be directing all her thoughts and energy toward the search for Tony did nothing to diminish the reality that Sam Wonder was undressing only a closed door away. Before she did anything else, Trina hurried to splash cool water on her face.

Because of its spontaneity, the evening took on a fairy-tale quality, with Sam Wonder the epitome of Prince Charming. She had never seen him dressed in anything besides jeans, except that one night in his hot tub when he'd substituted cutoffs. He was one of those males for whom denim and boots had been invented.

Of course, he looked equally good in the navy sports jacket and gray pleated slacks he'd picked up that afternoon.

Trina was glad she had passed up the more conservative two-piece beige outfit on the grounds that it resembled something from her old wardrobe. In her dark chintz dress with its ruffled, off-the-shoulder neckline, fitted waist, and full skirt, she felt sophisticated and feminine and alluring.

Drinking champagne from a fluted stem while listening to piano music didn't do any damage to the illusion, either. And strolling hand in hand with a tall, handsome man whose attention never strayed from her was heady stuff. She let herself surrender to the magic.

Dinner at one of the city's best restaurants in a downtown hotel was a feast for both eye and palate. Business in any form did not intrude on their conversation, nor did the implications of their afternoon appointment. Instead, they concentrated on each other.

By the time they had finished dessert, a sampler of four different kinds of decadence, Trina was completely enthralled. From literally holding her hand as he helped her put her plans into action to ensuring that they have a delightful meal, Sam had made this day nearly perfect.

She smiled across the booth at him. "Thank you."

"You're welcome. For what?"

"Everything. Sara, coming with me, this." Her hand made a sweep of the burnished wood luxury of their surroundings. "I know you planned it all as a distraction."

His brows lifted. "I just wanted to share some of the places I like, and for you to enjoy them."

"I did." Her thumb and index finger slid up and down the stem of her liqueur glass before she brought it to her lips for the final sip. "What would you like to do next?"

"I'd like to go back to the hotel and make love."

Trina was thankful she'd already swallowed the last of her drink. "Just like that?" she asked, snapping her fingers.

"Well, no. I'd want it to last a little longer than that," he replied with an echoing snap.

"You're doing it again."

"I'm not doing anything." A smile played with the corners of his mouth. "Yet."

"Yes, you are. You keep making these bold statements of where you stand and what you want. That puts the burden of decision on me."

He gave the waiter a discreet signal for the check. "What else can I do? I've made up my mind. Now all I can do is wait for you to do the same. I never said I wouldn't try to influence you."

"We've known each other just three weeks, Sam. I'm not used to moving so fast."

"Three weeks if you go by the calendar. But total the time we've spent together, and it'll probably amount to more than the average couple sees each other in six months. You know everything about my business, we have fun, and we can tolerate each other across the table three meals a day. Plenty of married people don't have that much togetherness."

"I hadn't thought of it in those terms." They not only worked side by side all day, they spent the bulk of their off-hours the same way. "It does add up to a lot."

And every minute had been building to this point. In a short span of time, Trina's feeling for Sam had deepened from initial attraction to something far more substantial and complex. The next step was inevitable.

She placed her napkin next to her plate and watched while Sam did a quick tally of the tab and slipped some bills in the portfolio. Without another word they stood, left the restaurant, and got into the car to drive back to the hotel.

Trina's stomach was alive with the usual flutters, though on another level she felt totally calm and assured. She supposed that came from accepting one's fate.

"I can't stand the silence or the suspense. Just tell me if you're thinking about it, at least." Sam had discarded the jacket and tie, and freed the top two buttons of his shirt, and looked exactly right at the wheel of her car.

"You mean, as in debating whether I want to or not?"

"Yes."

"No. I'm not thinking about that."

"Oh." He downshifted for a light with savage efficiency.

"What I can't *stop* thinking about is how good it's going to be. And how I can't wait. You told me to think long and hard, remember? And I have."

He stared at her, eyes wide, clearly astonished. The signal turned green, and behind them, a horn blared. Sam tore off like a drag racer until he spotted a place to pull over. His right hand clamped on her shoulder. "Trina, the line was perfect, but your timing needs work."

"I should have waited to tell you? I got the feeling you were rather anxious to know."

He swore under his breath. "I did want to know. But will you hold off on any more bombshells until I can turn this thing over to valet parking? I'd hate like hell having to explain why I wrapped it around a parking meter."

Trina managed to keep quiet except for the most superficial exchanges until they reached her room. But as they rode up in the elevator, her eyes were gleaming with promises, and so were Sam's. She hadn't exaggerated when she'd said she couldn't wait.

Once inside, they didn't turn on any lamps, but drew open the drapes instead. The softer, diffused light allowed other senses to prevail.

In front of the window they faced each other, almost touching. Sam lowered his head slightly; she felt his breath on her neck beneath her ear. "You're wearing a different perfume. Did you buy it today?"

"Yes. I picked it with you in mind."

"If you meant to seduce me, it's working. You probably didn't have to bother. Just smelling *you* would have the same effect."

Trina trembled and went up on her toes, grazing his neck with her lips. "I know. It's the same for me. You smell hot. That's the second thing I noticed about you the day I showed up at your house. It makes me hot too."

She heard his swift intake of breath, saw his chest rise. "You're one surprise after another tonight. I'm not used to you saying stuff like that, but don't stop. Tell me how you feel. Show me everything you want."

His mouth covered hers. Gently, skillfully, but with complete authority, he slid his tongue between her lips, then stilled, inviting her to do with it what she would.

Feeling daring enough to be brazen, she sucked. Once.

He groaned, and the kiss quickly became ravenous, a fiery, passionate race to taste and absorb everything at once. Their tongues circled and rubbed and mated, infinitely curious and insatiably hungry.

Still devouring her mouth, Sam bowed his back and began unbuttoning his shirt. The widening V of exposed chest drew Trina's hands like a magnet. Her palms moved in airy circles over his well-defined pecs, and his nipples hardened into tight beads, just as hers were doing with only the expectation of contact.

His shirt fluttered to the floor, and he dragged her hands to his bare shoulders, then curved his over her collarbones. "All night you've teased me with this dress. Is that ruffle the only thing holding it up?"

"That's all." She loved the way his chest hair tickled the underside of her tongue and the rush of power she felt when his muscles rippled.

"So with one tug, I could feel your breasts next to me? Skin to skin?"

She swayed, caught in the sensual snare of Sam's words. Some allusions were just too evocative. "With one tug."

"Do it for me, Trina. Now."

The hoarse command galvanized her. Wantonly she pulled the elastic outward and down so that it shaped and lifted her, an invitation and a plea. "For you."

He shuddered and hissed an oath. His hands cupped her, and while his fingers gently kneaded her fullness, he whispered promises that his mouth would soon bestow even greater pleasure.

Just being this close to him, half-dressed, filled Trina with an aching need that was almost painful. She wasn't sure she could bear more of Sam's brand of pleasure. His lips closed around just the tip of one breast, and she felt herself growing taut from the heat of his possession. Gradually he opened wider to draw more of her in, to dampen her with his flicking tongue and temper her nipple with the gentle scrape of his teeth. The strong, wet suction of his flexing cheeks made Trina bite her lip to keep from whimpering.

By the time he began ravishing her other breast, his mouth had turned greedier, his technique less practiced, his hands shakier. He was losing control, and she reveled in it. She didn't want to be the only one undone by this glorious agony.

Then he crushed her against him, melding her softness with the unyielding resistance of his abdominal muscles. In that instant the full impact of being a woman hit Trina—the marvelous differences between male and female that enabled them to take from and give to each other. "Oh, Sam, you're so hard."

"That's no lie, Kat-a-rina." She had been referring to his chest, but the term applied to the rest of him as well. Hard everywhere. He fused their lips in a kiss so wild, so blazing, so carnal in its intent that she swayed again and clamped her hands on his waist, certain her legs couldn't support her much longer.

Propelled by a timeless instinct, they had drifted toward the bed. Sam kicked off his shoes and socks;

Trina discarded her sandals, glad she'd decided against wearing stockings this evening. He unclasped his belt but hesitated, questioning her with his eyes.

Surely he didn't think she would change her mind at this point. Trina nodded and reached behind her. Each downward click of her zipper matched his, setting off little bursts of warmth inside her.

And then they stood face-to-face, stripped of everything but their unrestrained desire for each other. She quelled the urge to let her gaze run rampant over him, all of him. Instead, her eyes locked with his. At last, as if he'd read her mind, he said huskily, "Go ahead. I want you to look."

She took quick advantage of the liberty he'd granted. The muscles she had admired so often were not his only impressive masculine attribute. Sam, fully aroused, would inspire even the most reserved lady to forget her good intentions. "You're every woman's fantasy."

"And you are mine."

She loved the way his voice thickened with desire, loved the avid way his eyes devoured her. "I'm glad you're so tall," she murmured, feathering her fingertips over his cheek.

"We'll fit perfectly." The flat of his hand moved up her outer thigh, smoothed over the hip, and rested in the dip of her waist. "I'm glad your legs are long."

"Mmm," she agreed, snuggling into the enveloping circle of his embrace. "Makes things easier."

He thrust his hips forward, branding her with

the magnitude of his need, while his fingers un-
erringly delved into the heart of hers.

She heard herself cry out, stunned by how her
body had quickened and flowered to receive him.
As if she'd been ready forever. Waiting for Sam to
take her.

"Trina, I want you. I'd like to make this last a
real long time. But I think I'm going to need a
second chance to do that." He sealed her lips with
his and bent to lift her.

"Sam, wait. I need to go to the bathroom."

He jerked upright. "You do?" He sounded annoyed.

"It's my— I have to put—" She could feel herself
flush. "We can't—"

"Can we save that till next time and let me take
care of this one?"

It was so tempting. "No, my way. I want to feel
all of you."

He groaned; his body quaked. "Then make it
fast, honey. 'Cause all of me feels like Vesuvius,
ready to erupt."

Trina gathered up her tote and hurried to the
bathroom. She probably took twice as long as
necessary, as much from eagerness as lack of
practice. When she finished and reached for the
doorknob, she hesitated. Could she stride back to
Sam nude? No, she wasn't quite that uninhibited
yet. Snatching her robe from the back of the door,
she shrugged into it.

He had stretched out on the bed, but even
though he was in the shadows and half-covered
by a sheet, she could see that his readiness hadn't
diminished.

"Get rid of the robe," he said, lifting the sheet to welcome her back into the haven of his arms. "You won't be needing it for a long time."

She dropped the filmy wrapper, and he tumbled her down beside him. His body was like an inferno, and his hands swept over every inch of her, arousing, demanding, spreading the flames. Trina arched and twisted, ascending the passionate spiral until she could go no higher without him.

She guided him into the hot, sheathing sanctuary of her femininity, gasping as he entered and filled her. "Sam!"

"Trina."

Verbal communication ceased, save for his name and hers, each repetition adding to the unbridled urgency of their shared desire.

She wanted, needed, to ensure Sam's satisfaction, but his hands were stroking, his tongue echoing the driving power of his hips, caressing her and claiming her. Consuming her.

It was like a tidal wave rising within her, each successive swell stronger and more insistent, building, climbing until it crashed around her. "Sam? I can't—" Oh, but, yes, she could, she could. . . .

Sam was swept into the maelstrom. No longer able to subdue his body's demands, he buried his face in the pillow next to Trina's head to muffle the raw sounds of his release. But her fists in his hair dragged his mouth over hers, opening to swallow his incoherent words of passion.

He was drowning in her, driven beyond reason to the edge of consciousness. Inside his head, her name reverberated, over and over, but he was past saying it. His untamed shout poured into her mouth as she claimed the ultimate testimony of his surrender.

Panting, shuddering, suspended at the pinnacle, he felt the sweet pulses of Trina's inner contractions, heard her sigh his name one last time, and he rocketed to the heights again.

Seven

Satiated and exhausted, they fell asleep wrapped around each other, the drapes still open. But dawn came early in June, and Trina woke at first light.

Close beside her, Sam sprawled on his stomach like a great golden bear. One arm anchored her midsection to the bed; his leg trapped both her ankles. And the sheet didn't conceal enough to keep her mind from wandering back to the previous night. Magical from beginning to end.

Her lack of restraint had come as a bit of a shock, yet she suffered neither embarrassment nor regret for anything she'd said or done, though most of it transcended the bounds of prior experience. But, then, she had never been with Sam before, never dealt with emotions as powerful as those he inspired.

He mumbled something, shifted onto his back, and flung an arm over his eyes. Trina held her breath until he resettled into the steady rhythm of sleep. She wanted time to herself to savor the memories.

Yesterday, she'd taken two giant steps, both symbolic of the changes her life was undergoing, both fraught with uncertainty. If Sara was successful, Trina would be able to regain the family she yearned for desperately. For nearly two months she had grappled with the specter of failure. Now she had a glimmer of hope, and she clung to it.

What she was going to do about Sam was more complicated. Given what lay ahead of her, spending the night with him had been a reckless indulgence. She had no business starting a relationship when they both knew their time together could be measured in days.

Was she brave—or foolish—enough to act the hedonist and wring the most out of each one?

In her entire life Trina had never been either reckless or indulgent, and no amount of talk about changing, no flashy car or new wardrobe, could alter such an ingrained pattern. *Trina, be a good girl and . . .* Her father would begin the sentence that way, then tell her what to do. Since she was unfailingly obedient, it had to follow that she was a good girl.

Sam had told her the same thing last night, more than once, using different words. Her mouth tipped up at the corners when she looked at his, which was diabolically attractive, even when slackened by sleep. Of course, his definition of good was a far cry from Anton's.

He stirred, gathering her to him. "Come 'ere," he

slurred, tangling their arms and legs, arranging her along the length of him. "'S better." Satisfied with her new position, he let out a sigh and fell silent again, leaving Trina to wonder if he'd been awake at all.

It thrilled her to know that he wanted her near, whether he was conscious of it or not.

Yes, she had changed enough to enjoy every remaining day with Sam, and to consign misery and remorse to the future. Within minutes, she was asleep again too.

A few hours later, Sam was pleading starvation. By the time they made it to the hotel restaurant, he put a rush on their order and asked the server to bring him something, anything, to munch on in the meantime. His appetite was impressive indeed. Just being around him whetted her own.

Their meals were delivered, and they ate in easy silence for a few minutes before she said, "At the risk of getting the same answer you gave me last night, what do you want to do today?"

Sam looked up from his he-man breakfast. "I think you're safe from that for a while." He grinned, or maybe leered. "Got to stoke the furnace if I intend to keep my . . . performance level up."

He was so bad! Tossing out his innuendoes when they both knew he hadn't had any problems in that area, either throughout the night or this morning. That's why they were so late. His "performance" had exceeded by several times the second chance he'd claimed to need.

No other man had ever been able to make her blush like a Victorian maiden. This one made a habit of it. "I refuse to touch that. Stoke your furnace if you need to, but don't expect me to stroke your ego."

His grin turned into a laugh. She'd just fed him a straight line, and could tell exactly what was going through his head.

Trina speared a wedge of papaya and shook it at him threateningly. "Don't you dare come back with anything that has to do with stroking. What is it about the male of the species that makes him so fond of sexual allusions?"

Sam pointed a crisp bacon strip at her before crunching half of it in one bite. "Probably our territorial instincts," he said with suspicious blandness. "Teasing with sexual allusion implies a certain familiarity. If a woman lets us get away with it, even though she scolds and acts offended, it's another form of claim-staking."

She choked down her papaya and sputtered, "That is without a doubt the most archaic rationale I've ever heard."

His green eyes glittered, but not with amusement. "Don't you know, Trina? A lot of men are throwbacks when it comes to the women they're personally involved with."

Personally involved—a perfect portrait of her. In every way, including the most personal of all, she was involved with Sam Wonder.

She chewed and swallowed her last bite of mixed fruit. "Back to my original question about our agenda."

"Looks like it's going to come a gully washer any second now." He grimaced and scratched his head, as if pondering a thorny problem. "Guess we'll be forced to spend the day inside."

She rolled her eyes, the typical womanly reaction he'd just described. "I knew all that fat and cholesterol would trigger your baser instincts."

"Ouch! Judged guilty even when my motives are pure." He signed the ticket on their room but left a generous cash tip, something he never failed to do, she'd noticed. "I meant," he explained, pulling her to her feet with both hands, "that we'll take an excursion right here inside Union Station. Lots of good stuff to keep us busy."

Trina would never own up to her energy being depleted, but leisurely browsing tantalized her more than yesterday's vigorous sightseeing. "Sounds perfect."

He bent to confide in her ear, "Say the word when you get tired. I can whisk you back to the room for a nap in two minutes flat."

She gave him a playful push. "You're *too* generous."

Stone-serious, he said, "I'll give you all you want, Trina. Remember that."

His cryptic remark might have been yet another sexy suggestion. Or it could have more far-reaching implications. Either way, she trembled.

Sam guided her to the walking tour, and Trina read every word of the first few plaques. When she realized Sam was reciting the same information in his own words, along with humorous asides, she gave up reading in favor of listening to his narration.

"You must have done this so often you have it memorized." Maybe it was a routine stop when he entertained women from out of town.

"For as long as I can remember, I've been fascinated by trains. The first summer my parents allowed me to ride to Kansas City alone, to visit relatives, I was convinced I'd become a man of the world. I was all of twelve." His eyes were shining with youthful enthusiasm.

"I'll never forget talking to the conductor, counting out my money for a truly awful lunch sandwich, and walking the whole length of the train, swaying every step. It was great."

A strange excitement coursed through Trina. At the bottom of her tote, smudged from repeated perusal, was a color brochure for the exotic Orient Express. London to Istanbul. The entire route. Her dream. Her fantasy. "I love trains too. Always have, though I haven't a clue as to why."

"I like to think it's in my blood." Sam meshed his fingers with hers. "Quite a few Wonders have worked on the railroads over the last hundred years. From cutting logs for ties to being executives, and doing most everything in between."

"You must feel a sense of continuity knowing your ancestors might have stood right here." She heard the pensiveness in her voice, and swallowed against an unfamiliar tightness in her throat.

His grip tightened. "Are you thinking about Tony being all you have?"

"Not really. I just can't help envying how you're steeped in your family. You live your life on your grandparents' land. Your parents are a phone call or a few hours away, ready to lend support for whatever you decide to do. You have myriad aunts, uncles, and cousins within driving distance, whom you see often."

"You make me sound like an ineffectual wimp,

unable to function without some relatives standing by."

She clutched his arm. "No, no. I didn't mean that at all. It's kind of hard to explain." She removed her hand and stared at it. "I guess the best way to put it is that because they *are* behind you, you rarely need to call on them. Your strength stems from knowing they're there. You're very lucky."

He steered her to a bench and dropped down beside her. "Do you feel unlucky? That no one's there for you?"

Trina wished she could stop obsessing about Sam's family and his place in the world. It invariably opened the door on a cavernous void in her own life. But she couldn't hold back the longing. "I know you get tired of listening to me bemoan my fate. It just seems so unfair that my one family connection decided to desert me."

Sam looked skeptical. "Are you taking this personally now, Trina? Claiming that Tony deserted *you*?"

"Of course not," she asserted. "I've explained why I think he left—that he couldn't coexist with our father."

"Still, you must feel like he abandoned you to a fate he wasn't strong enough to endure. Left you to tough it out alone when a big brother is supposed to be protective."

"That's ridiculous!" Indignation gave her voice a sharp edge. "My parents were not evil monsters."

"So you say. But it takes something pretty monstrous to send a seventeen-year-old running away to nothing."

Trina scrambled to her feet, too agitated to remain immobile. She strode over to stare at the toy display in a shop window. In the glass she could see Sam's tall reflection behind her.

"If only he'd tried to meet Papa halfway, but, no, he had to be pigheaded about every trivial thing. He was smart, a lot smarter than I am, and could have excelled in school. But would he do that? No way, because that's what Papa stressed. I did it, and things didn't turn out so badly."

"Maybe he just got fed up with having your example thrown in his face and decided to hell with it."

She whirled and planted her fists on his chest. "How dare you accuse me of being responsible!"

His hands closed over hers, pinning them. "I wasn't leveling an accusation, Trina. Merely suggesting a possibility. You were the perfect, dutiful daughter, he the rebellious son. Don't you suppose your father pointed out that disparity with some frequency?"

Her anger disintegrated, and she laid her forehead on his chest, between their joined hands. "You're right. Hardly a day passed that he didn't berate Tony for not being more like me. I hated hearing it, but what was I supposed to do? Start acting like he did? I'm not sure I could have done that, even if I'd wanted to."

Sam wrapped an arm around her waist while he smoothed her hair with a hand. "You never say much about your mother's role in all this. Couldn't she have intervened? Played peacemaker?"

"That sounds like the logical solution. But you have to remember, my parents were very Old

World in that respect. Much as they wanted to embrace America and its ways, they were still bound by Eastern European tradition. Which dictated that the man ruled his family."

She felt Sam nod. "So everybody ended up a victim, including your father. He lost his only son forever. I can't believe he didn't suffer because of it."

"If he did, he kept his pain inside. He never relented, even on his deathbed. He refused to say Tony's name." She shook her head. "Such obstinate, useless pride. I often wonder if distance helped Tony see the error of Papa's ways. They were so much alike. It'd be a shame for that stubbornness to afflict another generation."

"Maybe you'll get a chance to see for yourself before long. Sara's good, Trina. I think she can find him."

"Thank you. Again." He was so good at saying what it took to cheer her out of a dark mood.

"No thanks necessary. Now what do you say we get this tour back on track?"

"You're on."

They watched three short features in the Memories Theater, hit the bookstore at Trina's insistence and the lingerie shop at Sam's. She managed to drag him out before he'd thoroughly embarrassed her, but not before she could prevent him buying a blush-pink teddy. Surprisingly he refrained from making the expected provocative comment, just winked and grinned smugly. The message was clear. Later.

It had been at least two hours since their last meal, and there was no keeping him away from the Fudgery. Caught up in the frivolity of flying marshmallows and nuts, along with candymakers doubling as singers and dancers who demanded audience participation, they pigged out on butter pecan and rocky road fudge.

When they returned to the hotel, Sam led her to the gilded arch that spanned the main entrance. He positioned her so that she faced one of the bases and told her to stay put. Then he moved to the opposite side, at least forty feet away.

In a soft, raspy voice he said, "Kat-a-rina, thinking of you in that teddy has made me real horny. Is there anything you can do about it?"

Trina's mouth dropped open; she whipped around to see how many people had overheard his outrageous request. No one acted as if anything were amiss, but she stormed over to Sam and said, "You rat! I'll have your hide for that."

"That's the idea, honey. Can you have it in a hurry?"

Sam lazed on a poolside lounge a few hours later. From beneath half-closed lids, he observed his father fiddling with the barbecue grill. He would putter endlessly, adding briquets, rearranging them, squirting on more lighter fluid to make a hotter fire, until he got it just right.

Like most men, Robert was near helpless in the kitchen, but slap tongs or a spatula in his hands, and he was transformed into an accomplished patio chef. This was a ritual they'd played out countless weekends while Sam was growing up, one he had taken for granted.

Trina's fixation on his family and her lack of one had forced him to view it in a different light. To her, it was a precious tradition he ought to treasure. Calling his parents had been her idea in the first place. Sam had balked because he knew it would mean a dinner invitation when he wanted—selfishly—to monopolize Trina. But she'd jumped at the chance with such childlike eagerness, he hadn't the heart to refuse.

Besides, he was feeling so magnanimous he'd probably give her anything she asked for. Just as she had given him exactly what he'd wanted that afternoon in their hotel room. A lazy smile split his lips, and his eyes drifted shut. Everything he wanted, and more. Damn! He hadn't felt this good in . . . Truth was, he couldn't recall *ever* feeling this good. Even when he was young and foolish.

That fact ought to be worrying him, but he preferred to put off examining it as long as possible.

"You're looking awfully pleased with yourself," Robert said, intruding on his unfolding daydream.

"Mmm," Sam agreed noncommittally.

"But since I swore not to interfere in your love life, I'll try to curb my natural curiosity."

"Trina and I came to St. Louis for business. On a whim, we decided to stay the night. I thought she'd get a kick out of the hotel at Union Station." He felt no obligation to disclose that had been yesterday.

His father ambled over to an adjoining lounge, bringing with him the smell of charcoal smoke that activated Sam's taste buds. "So the work with Trina is progressing well?"

Sam noticed that Robert deliberately made it sound as if they were partners in a joint project. "We're getting there. She's sharp, comes up with all kinds of innovative ideas, and not just on the money end of things."

"I'd never say 'I told you so,' but she did come highly recommended."

Sam let that pass. He knew the old meddler had fallen back, but wasn't about to concede defeat. "She's on her way to California, you know."

"So she said." Robert scanned the backyard, pride and contentment reflected in his features. Other than the pool, he and Sam's mother had done every bit of the elaborate landscaping, including the fish pond. "Don't know what she expects to find there, but I suspect it won't be what she's really looking for."

"Since when did you turn philosophical?"

"Doesn't take philosophy to tap into her restlessness. There's something missing in her life, and she hasn't yet decided what it is, much less how to get it."

Trina was dead certain that finding Tony would supply the magical missing link that would put her fragmented life back together. Sam was inclined to agree with his father. Whatever she needed would have to come from within herself.

It was a lesson he'd learned ten years ago, one nobody else had been able to teach him.

"She's a grown woman, and smart. She ought to be able to figure it out sooner or later." He planted one foot on the pool apron, swinging his knee. "I don't have the answer. And if I tried to tell her I did, she'd probably tell me where to stick my opinion. She's real sensitive about anyone controlling her."

"Samson, my boy, it's hard to know what women want these days. Come on too strong, they accuse you of trying to dominate them. Stand back and let them do their thing, they complain you don't care." He shook his head. "Things were simpler in my day."

"So what does a man do?"

"Play your instincts and hope to strike the right balance. Luckily it works often enough to ensure the propagation of the human race."

Sam wasn't ready to deal with propagating or anything else that permanent, not while nursing the sick fear in his gut that Trina might fly away on a moment's notice, and that nothing he could do would stop her. After last night he was afraid he might try, and Lord knew what would happen then. "I'm in too deep," he said in a harsh undertone. His knee swung faster.

If Robert heard that, he pretended not to. "Son, your mother is very fond of Trina."

"What's that supposed to mean?" As if he didn't know. Both of his parents approved of her and wanted to send the message loud and clear.

"It means," Robert said, eyes twinkling like Saint Nick's, "that your mother is very fond of Trina." Left unspoken was the implication that, as hard as they'd tried not to interfere, neither of them had believed Marianne was the right woman for Sam.

"Try not to get your hopes up too high, Dad. We've a long road ahead of us." Sam wondered if perhaps he hadn't said that as much for himself as for his father.

"I always have high hopes," Robert said. "It's what keeps life interesting." He stood and went back to check his fire. "This looks just right to sear some steaks. Let's see if our ladies have everything under control in the kitchen."

His lady, Sam mused idly, following his father. Trina could be that for sure, and he liked it. She could also be a naughty wanton, as he'd repeatedly found out. He liked that even better.

He began plotting an early conclusion to their visit.

"What can I do to help?" Trina asked, watching Natalie Wonder dump assorted vegetables into one of the double sinks.

"There's some melted butter on the stove. Smush this clove of garlic in it and spread it on those Italian bread slices." With brisk efficiency she thrust a metal garlic press at Trina. "Then you can wash that romaine. Sam loves Caesar salad. Here's some Parmesan you can grate."

How different this was from her mother's kitchen, where she'd been forbidden to lift a finger. Here she was treated like everyone else. "It was nice of you to invite us on such short notice."

"My dear, Sam grew up in this house. He and his friends have never needed an invitation to eat here. I was always prepared for extras, and there were always plenty of them. We encouraged it. In every neighborhood there seems to be a place where all the kids congregate. This was it."

Different, too, from the Bartok's regimented household where studying and serious artistic pursuits were emphasized more than socializing with friends. "It must have been difficult getting used to the quiet when Sam left home."

"Heavens, I never had time. The same week he went away to the university, a good friend and I began planning the business we were going to start."

Trina shook the last lettuce leaf and dropped it in the colander. It was astonishing to derive this much satisfaction from such a mundane chore. "What sort of business do you have?"

"Victorian Brides is the name," Natalie said proudly. "We specialize in reproductions of period wedding gowns, or occasionally the real thing, if we've been fortunate enough to find one."

"How delightful and . . . romantic."

The older woman chuckled. "Our husbands thought we were crazy, I think, but we believed there was a demand for what we wanted to provide. To their credit, they supported us in every possible way. In reality we suspected they were merely indulging us through menopause." She laughed outright at that, as if it were an absurd notion.

"I hope you proved them wrong on all counts."

"Indeed we did. We keep two seamstresses busy full time, and several others help out during the busiest times. We've exceeded even our own ambitions."

Trina paused, cheese in one hand and grater in the other. "I hate to confess this, but when we met, I stereotyped you as the traditional housewife. You were such a gracious hostess, your home so lovely and warm, I figured you must devote full time to it."

"Well, I did do that for years, and I still take pride in those things." She pointed an admonishing finger at Trina. "Not because it's what I'm supposed to do, but because I actually enjoy cooking and gardening and entertaining our friends and Robert's business associates.

"I know you young career women find those things objectionable and unworthy of your intelligence, but I simply don't agree."

"No, I— It isn't that I object to women doing them." In this instance it was Trina who felt inadequate and lacking. "I just never learned how." She related the reason to Natalie, adding, "I have Mama's cookbook, recipes she wrote down in longhand. I've always imagined myself capable of whipping up some of those scrumptious dishes to serve company. Maybe someday I'll get around to it."

"I'm sure you will, dear. Good cooking is not an inherent talent. It comes from practice, like any other skill." The older woman examined a yellow squash, then with a knife and several deft additions of other bits of vegetables, turned it into a goose with carrot feet.

Trina watched her attach a tiny red cabbage bow tie. "How clever. Where did you learn that?"

Natalie smiled sheepishly. "When I stayed home, I took every kind of course imaginable." She held up the decorated squash. "Garnishes. I also dabbled in flower arranging, napkin folding, wok cookery, and several dozen more. I'm not one for soap operas and bridge clubs."

"No, I see that you're not." Trina went back to her grating while she debated how to bring up something that had been puzzling her about Sam's relationship with his father. Before she had a chance, the men came trooping in from the patio.

"You've got a couple of hungry hombres here," Robert announced. "We're ready when you are."

Trina's gaze flew to Sam's. He looked hungry, all right. Ready too. Her heartbeat did its usual number. He'd had that effect on her since her very first glimpse of him. Now it was keener, more deeply felt, and more meaningful.

Eager as she was to see him, she couldn't help regretting that she and Natalie had been interrupted. Trina had warmed to the quiet pleasure of exchanging girl talk and small confidences in the cozy surroundings. There was just something about a kitchen that drew her.

Robert hefted the platter holding five thick rib eyes. "Come on, Son. Let's tend to men's work."

They ate on the shady rock-walled patio, a burbling fountain and songbirds providing background music. In spite of Sam's fervent looks and veiled hints about how late it was getting, Trina had never spent a more pleasant evening. Though it was unspoken, these three people shared an obvious abundance of warmth and acceptance and love. Instead of wallowing in depression because she was an outsider, Trina luxuriated in the circle of Sam's family.

"Thank you for taking me," she told him later in the car on their way back to the hotel. "I had a wonderful time." She found herself using that adjective far too often in matters relating to Sam.

"Give yourself the credit. It was your idea."

"Yes, I know." She sighed, snuggling into the sheepskin seatcovers. "But you didn't fight it too hard."

"I might have if I hadn't sensed you really wanted to go." He reached over and squeezed her thigh with the familiarity of someone who had done it often enough to be sure of its acceptance. "I'd have been satisfied with . . . room service."

"Maybe for breakfast, hmm?" Trina purred seductively, knowing they weren't talking about food.

"Maybe tonight, too, hmm?"

"How can I turn down such generosity?"

Trina woke in an empty bed, but the scent of Sam lingered. She savored it as she slowly reentered consciousness. A slow savoring. That's what last night had been. And on a different level it had surpassed the one before. With their urgency slaked, she and Sam had taken time to discover the nuances of lovemaking, an exquisite unraveling of all the senses that had culminated in a fulfillment so profound it left them shattered, and awed.

In her heart Trina understood that she would never find that fulfillment with anyone but Sam. Nor would she want to. Sam was magic, strange and tender as the "Mr. Wonderful" lyrics claimed. The thrill and the glow were there too. A generation earlier, the song had been written for a man like him.

She sat up and snagged her robe off the floor. First things first, and that meant a shower.

Trina stepped into the bathroom, then slammed her back against the door, as if someone had knocked the breath out of her. Ribbons of heat slithered up her legs, unfurled in her belly, streamed over her breasts.

Erotic. Visceral. Sexy. Evocative. No word was powerful enough to describe the way Sam affected her body at that moment.

Facing the full-wall mirror, his bare back to her, jeans unzipped and riding low, he stood while he scraped a straight razor over his lathered face. It was such a purely masculine act that it shot to her feminine core like a bullet.

"Trina? What is it?"

She reacted without thinking, pressing against his back, kissing his shoulder blades, letting her hands roam rapaciously over his chest, and lower. If she could have devoured him, she would have. "I'm crazy about your bones."

Silent laughter rippled in his chest as he bent to rinse off the lather. "Yeah? I kinda like yours too."

"No, I mean literally, your bone structure. The way your jawline stands out, the little dent in your chin, those hollows under your cheekbones, the sharp nose, how your neck cords strut. And best of all, that groove above your lips that tastes almost as good as it looks." As she listed each feature, she touched it with the pad of her index finger. "You are a man women will always want to look at."

Turning, he took her in his arms. "I don't have

any control over *women* looking. But make no mistake, Trina. I'm a one-woman man. Always have been."

He proceeded to prove it, and they got a very late start driving back.

Eight

Trina hung up the phone, let out a muted squeal of delight, and rode her executive chair on a complete spin. She'd just finished a preliminary call to the head of an investors' syndicate in New York, a group she'd had some dealings with during her banking days. She had pitched the basics of the Chimera project, though not by name or place, and he'd been interested enough to tell her to put together some figures and get back to him.

She was pleased with herself and hoped Sam would be equally so. It was nearly four, and he hadn't set foot in the office all day. After sharing this space with him for several weeks, she'd got used to his presence.

Waking up beside him two mornings in a row shouldn't have been habit-forming. Yet the first thing she'd thought of today was her loneliness.

Her fault, entirely. Sam had been more than willing to drive straight to his house when they'd got back from St. Louis the night before. Barring that, he'd offered to stay in her room at the lodge, a major concession on his part, she was sure. It was acknowledged throughout the organization that if he had anything going with a woman, he handled it so discreetly no one had a clue as to whom she might be.

At her insistence they'd agreed not to advertise their relationship, but accomplishing that was going to be tricky. People around here weren't blind. Inwardly Trina felt like such a different person. There must be outward signs as well. Something had blossomed within her, a sense of fullness she'd never experienced before.

It overflowed frequently, like now, when she could feel a dreamy smile spreading over her face. She loved the feeling, but it could be a detriment to getting any work done.

She pawed through several stacks of paper, searching for the questions she'd jotted down regarding some numbers from the marketing department. Might as well walk up the hill to that office now and ask for clarification so she could get the final package worked up for New York.

At the same time she stepped out the lodge's main entrance, Sam pulled his Bronco up under the portico. "Hop in," he said through the open passenger window.

She did, without asking why or where, without sparing a thought to her original mission. All because she hadn't seen him for almost twenty-four hours.

"Where have you been hiding out today?" If she

didn't take care, she could see herself turning possessive, not a trait she aspired to.

"Spent all day up at the golf-course site where they're drilling a well. We're at two hundred feet now, and into rock. It's coming along."

Trina once again marveled that he stayed on top of every detail that involved the lodge's well-being. "And are you still on duty?" It was obvious they were heading away from Chimera.

He swept off the wide-brimmed Stetson he'd been wearing and sailed it into the backseat. "Nope. I'm changing into my other hat until tomorrow morning."

"Which hat is that?" she asked, aware of a slight catch in her voice. It probably resulted from the way he eyed her above-the-knee jumpsuit, as if he might run his hand up one of the full legs.

"The one where I see to your education and entertainment." She saw his brows climb above the dark sunglasses frames.

"You think I need education and entertainment?" He'd managed to do a pretty fair job of providing both so far.

Sam wheeled onto the main highway. "I think we all do. But first . . ." He stopped at the Lake Ozark Post Office and reached under the seat for an empty oversize manila envelope. "I'll only be a sec."

He returned, dropping the bulging envelope in her lap. "What's this?"

"An experiment of mine. Several years back, I had registration start running me a printout, with names and addresses of everyone who stayed at the lodge. Within a week of their stay I send them a guest-comment card asking for complaints, compliments, and suggestions."

"Most hotels put those directly in the rooms."

"Yeah, I know. But the response rate isn't all that great. And sometimes those that are filled out don't end up where they need to go."

They stopped at a busy highway intersection before Sam turned toward Camdenton. "You mean management doesn't want the owners to hear complaints, so they get conveniently rerouted or ignored?"

"Right. I decided to try a different tack, and I'm getting about a twenty-five percent return, which is outstanding for mail solicitation. More important, it helps me keep an eye on things as the customers see them."

"And if you see patterns repeated, somebody is in for either praise or reevaluation."

"You know, Trina, you've really caught on quick to how this business works. I've met hotel managers who don't have as clear a grasp of how it functions as you do."

Trina beamed at the compliment. She'd always prided herself on being a fast learner, but accolades from Sam meant something special. "Much of what I've picked up is just common sense."

"I know. But in my experience that's often a rare commodity in the business world."

Since they were on the subject of business, it seemed the perfect opportunity to bring up the plan she'd set in motion that day. "When I worked at the bank, we sometimes had clients who wanted to invest in, shall we say, non-traditional projects.

In these situations I often hooked them up with an investment syndicate."

"Mmm," he responded, not sounding particularly interested. "An investment syndicate being another name for a bunch of venture capitalists, I take it?"

"Yes, well, today I called up the head honcho of the one I dealt with most, and the Chimera expansion intrigued him. I'm getting together a prospectus."

"You're doing what?" he roared.

Trina repeated her whole speech, though she assumed the question was rhetorical. "Do you have some problem with that?"

"Yes, I have a major problem with that. In fact, first thing tomorrow, you can get on the horn and tell that guy thanks, but no thanks. This isn't negotiable, or even up for discussion."

His inflexibility shocked her. "I can vouch that this group has an excellent performance history. They have abundant financial resources, and thrive on finding creative ways to increase them."

"I don't give a rip if they've got the treasury of a Middle East sheikdom backing them. They are not coming in here and grabbing a chunk of Chimera."

Trina crossed her arms and turned sideways in her seat. "Perhaps you'd care to elaborate on that. I'm confused. Are we talking about the same thing?"

"Yes, we most assuredly are. But you may as well drop it right there. Talking about vultures like that is a sure-fire way to ruin my appetite."

"The most abominable of sins." She ran her

fingernail along the edge of the envelope in her lap, pondering. "In other words you have a bad taste for venture capitalists."

"You're being too polite."

"But why? What do you have against them in general?"

He rubbed the back of his neck. "Let's just say that I had a very narrow escape at the time of the first expansion. I let myself get tied up with a pack like that and damned near lost control of this place. I will never run that risk again."

She'd had this deal in the back of her mind from the beginning, but knowing how adamant Sam was about retaining complete control over Chimera, she could see that Plan A was dead in the water.

"Fair enough," she conceded. "It's a given that investors are not going to shower you with cash unless they cover their backsides."

"Well, they're not going to cover them with a piece of me," he declared, sounding very much the tough bargainer.

Time for Plan B. She suspected that implementing it wouldn't do his appetite any good either. "I've wondered why you needed a consultant in the first place. With Robert's connections he could have money in your bank within a few days, and probably on your terms."

"I'll grant you that would be the logical route to go. And, as you say, direct and fast."

What he *hadn't* said was the key, but she didn't know if it was worth pushing further. "Another dead issue, right?"

"Like I said, you catch on quick."

She might be bright, but she could also be as stubborn as any Missouri mule. "I don't see how you can lump your father with a bunch of vultures—your word."

Sam flipped on his turn signal at the big Bridal Cave sign. "Remember what you told me about your father trying to make all your decisions and control your life?"

"Yes." Surely he wasn't going to equate Robert's benign meddling with Anton's manipulation.

"When I wanted to build Chimera, I had to accept help from Dad. Nobody in their right mind would bankroll a twenty-seven-year-old who wanted to do something that hadn't been tried here before, and on a grand scale at that. This time it's important for me to do this strictly on my own."

She certainly understood how hot that need could burn. "The ultimate statement of independence?"

"Maybe. Dad tries really hard to remember that I'm a grown-up now. He does a better job of it when he isn't involved in my business. You can sympathize with how I feel, can't you?"

"Of course." So, they'd had their first job-related disagreement, if it could be called that, and emerged relatively unscathed. Trina hadn't fought all that hard for her cause. But even if she had, on this one matter, she knew Sam would always be unwavering.

He steered the Broncho into a half-filled lot and parked it. "All this heavy talk has got me overheated. Let's do the cave and see if I can get cooled off."

Trina had never been in a cave before. She wasn't convinced she wanted to be in this one. The public-television documentaries she'd seen didn't paint them as overly hospitable places.

"Are there bats in here?" she whispered to Sam while they stood in the reception area, awaiting the next tour.

"Don't worry," he whispered back. She could tell he was smiling. "It's a myth that they dive-bomb straight into your hair."

She shuddered and tightened the elastic securing her hair. "This is the season of summer storms. What if the electricity goes off?"

"All the guides carry emergency-power supplies."

Sam put his arm around her, and the jitters abated somewhat. It seemed years since he'd touched her.

"That's more like it," he sighed, feeling her relax against him. "I've gone too many hours without touching."

Way too many. "I'll second that." She tried to smile confidently at the ranger who would lead them into the earth's core where certain doom lurked. "It doesn't take much of a rock slide to close off passages and openings, does it?"

Sam shared a laugh with the guide. "Trust me, Trina. You'll be safer below ground than you were on the highway coming over here."

"I'm so reassured."

Despite her doubts, she forget her reluctance almost as soon as the guide began to disclose the history of what they would be seeing. Centuries before, Osage Indians had discovered the spectacular formations that lay **buried** beneath Thunder Mountain.

Local legend recounted an Indian wedding taking place inside the cave in the early nineteenth century, establishing a tradition that continued to the present day and inspired the modern name, Bridal.

They hung back a bit at the rear of the group. "You mean people still get married here?" she whispered again, charmed by the idea. One glance at the soaring wall of onyx had cured her forever of cave anxiety. Trina now saw Nature's majestic display as a cool, beautiful retreat into a world that conjured up visions of a fairyland castle.

"There is a wedding chapel, decorated with stalactites. They claim more than a thousand couples have taken the plunge here."

"Oh, don't be so unromantic," she scolded. "I think it's a lovely idea."

"I," he announced, snaking both hands around her waist from behind and pulled her tight against his front, "am feeling very romantic." He rotated his hips for emphasis. "I'll show you if you'll quit fretting about what people will say and come home with me tonight."

Trina had to face facts. She was addicted to Sam. And anytime he wanted her with him, it was practically impossible to refuse. Because she wanted the same thing.

"A compromise," Trina offered, after an argument in which Sam and Paige had ganged up on her. "I'll learn to drive the boat, but I will not get on those water skis. No way. Both of you just save your breath."

"You didn't want to go in a cave either, and look how much you like to now," Sam said with a smirk that made her want to kick him.

After her initiation in Bridal Cave two weeks ago, he'd dragged her to several others, each on private property, off-limits to all except them. Spelunking was one of Sam's hobbies, and he was quite proficient at it. Almost as adept as he was at seducing Trina in the still, shivery darkness, where he could inflame her senses until she begged. Fortunately she could put him at her mercy with the same ease.

Trina gave him her version of a smug smile and hopped off his covered dock into the boat. "Don't press your luck." But of course he would. She rarely won against Sam. He just kept coming at her, a human battering ram with boundless tenacity.

"Let's get this show on the road." Paige had paddled across the lake in one of the lodge's canoes, looking for some action, as she phrased it. Much as she protested the plan, Trina was glad for the diversion. Since Sara had called her three days ago about chasing a lead in California, she'd barely been able to think about anything else.

"Okay," Paige said, barking orders. "You ski this time, Sam. Trina can be observer, and I'll drive while I give her lessons." She never abandoned her schoolteacher's habits for long.

Trina sat in the passenger seat as bidden, watching Paige turn on the key and fiddle with the various gauges and instruments. "Boy, I mean! If

I had your Porsche and this boat, I could die a happy woman."

"But then you wouldn't be able to enjoy them," Trina pointed out, getting a kick out of Paige's vitality. She was only three years older than the other woman, but usually felt more like her mother. Paige reminded her of Peter Pan.

"Well, you know what I meant."

Sam retrieved lifebelts, skis, and a towrope from a locker, tossing two belts into the boat. Then he shucked off his jeans so unexpectedly and so fast, Trina's head jerked and her mouth fell open. In a matter of seconds he had plunged headfirst into the lake.

"You can close your mouth now," Paige said. "He's attaching the towrope." And so began her routine of explaining every detail that Trina would need to know to pilot the boat and pull a skier.

When Sam climbed the ladder back to the dock, water sluicing down that magnificent body, Trina was glad she only had to observe instead of being a responsible driver.

"Gonna take off from there?" Paige asked, starting the engine at Sam's nod. "Okay, let's do it." She reversed the boat and eased it out of the well. "I'm going to make a slow pass by, and you need to toss the coiled rope to Sam on the dock."

Trina did as told, feeling a bit like a simple-minded child. Sam didn't help matters by puckering his lips in a mock kiss. He really could be a smart aleck at times.

"Now," Paige went on, "I'm going to advance real slowly until we take up all the slack. Watch and tell me when Sam's hand goes down."

Again Trina performed on command, and Paige shifted into neutral. "Is he going to take off from sitting on the dock on only one ski?"

"Yep. Raise your hand and tell him we're ready."

Trina felt like an interpreter at the UN. "What's next?"

"Hit it!" Sam and Paige yelled simultaneously, and the boat shot forward in a burst of power. He came up smoothly and began an immediate cut to the outside.

"One of the most important things to remember, Trina, is when you take off, be sure the rope is tight and the skier straight behind the boat. Then accelerate fast and keep the speed constant unless your skier signals you otherwise."

Trina never took her eyes off Sam as they streaked along the deserted cove and into the main arm of the lake.

"What do you think?" Paige shouted over the motor's throb.

"His, umm, form is good."

Paige giggled. "Lots of folks notice that right away. Point to that cove on the right. If he wants to swing in there, he'll give you the sign."

"He says to do it," Trina relayed.

They made a wide turn, and Paige said, "No, I mean what do you *really* think?"

Trina fought to tame her whipping hair. She wasn't exactly outfitted for this sort of activity. "I *really* think his form is good."

Undaunted, Paige supplied her own unique twist. "I think the man's tumbled head over hindside for you."

Trina didn't take the bait, and she continued

with her analysis. "Let me tell you why. Sam never—I mean *never*—brings women, or much of anybody else to his house. He's kind of a hermit over here on his hillside."

Trina remembered his resentment when she'd blundered onto his turf that first day. But she'd returned many times by invitation. In fact, in the weeks since they'd got back from St. Louis, he'd been pressuring her to transfer her things to his place.

She hedged, not wanting to take that final step for a variety of reasons. "I'm very fond of him," she admitted, and heard Paige snort. Fond. What a white-bread euphemism for her feelings. Trina was too chicken to use the word "love," but she knew that was the only term that would suffice.

Paige's impish demeanor turned fierce. "Sam has undergone some drastic changes because of you, Trina. Believe it. And if you go trampling all over him, I'm going to come after you with a fileting knife. Believe that too."

Trina believed it. Trampling all over Sam was the last thing she'd ever want to do. But sometimes things happened, and people who didn't deserve it got hurt.

Sam skiied for a while, then Paige took a turn. She, too, had excellent form, but Trina's interest in it wasn't quite as rapt as it had been earlier.

Back at the dock, they cooked burgers on the grill, then Paige got ready to paddle off in her canoe again, chattering about hitting one of the local country-music clubs with a gang of lodge employees.

"Matt going along?" Sam asked innocently.

Trina gaped as Paige turned purple before her eyes.

"That skunk knows better than to come within spitting distance of me. I'll clean his clock quicker than he could beg me not to."

Sam shook his head. "I wish you two could quit snarling and clawing long enough to hash out your differences. Every year Matt turns ornerier and you get more bitchy."

"Well, Cousin, don't give any odds on that happening in this lifetime." She struck out with a vicious slap of her paddle.

"Whew, what was that about?"

"It's as much a mystery to me as it is to you. My best friend and favorite cousin haven't spoken each other's names in ten years. Other than the two of them, nobody seems to know what set it off."

He turned to face her, placing her arms around his torso, the way he liked them. "Want to go up and look at my etchings?" He nipped at her ear as incentive.

She pulled back. "You must have forgotten. I've been in every room of your house. There isn't a single etching."

"Surely I have something to interest you."

She bit one of his nipples. "I'll try to think of something on the way up the hill."

But the phone was ringing when they opened the door, and since very few people had Sam's unlisted number, he picked it up. Trina could tell from the wary way he said "Yes" after the caller identified himself that it was not a call he particularly wanted to take. She ducked into the half bath to comb her hair and give him some privacy.

When she returned to the den, he'd hung up but hadn't stepped away from the phone. "Everything okay?" she asked, though she could divine the answer from the set of his shoulders.

"It was Sara."

"Oh," Trina said plaintively, knowing she wasn't going to like what he had to tell her. "She didn't want to talk to me?"

He turned to face her, his expression unreadable. "I told her it would be better if you heard it from me."

"I see." She felt herself wilting, felt the strength seeping out of her legs, and plopped into the nearest chair.

"It didn't amount to anything, Trina. It was a bum lead, a false trail. Not Tony."

Arms crossed in front of her, Trina folded in on herself. She would not fall apart. Hadn't Sara and Sam and her own logic warned her the man in California was a long shot? But he'd been the only promising clue on that front, and she had hoped. So much hope. Wasted.

"I wanted it to be him," she said in a voice from somewhere far away.

Sam came toward her. "I know you did, honey. But don't give up. Sara isn't." He stood in front of her now, so tall and invincible. So absolutely certain of where he belonged, when she belonged nowhere. Had no one.

Trina bounded to her feet, bolting for the front door. If she could get in her car and fly, she could leave the nightmare behind her.

He allowed her only a few steps before his hand clamped her arm like a vise. "There's no point in running, Trina. It'll be with you wherever you go."

"You don't understand how I feel, Sam. How this hurts." She abhorred the tremor in her voice, the way her bottom lip quivered against her will.

"That's right." He didn't let go. "I've never been in the position you're in right now, so I don't know how you feel, how you hurt. Does that mean I can't feel for you, hurt for you?"

She crumpled into his arms, hating to expose her weakness but needing his reassurance too much to do otherwise. "Tony's not in California. That's where I was going, and now there's no use. He isn't there."

"He has to be somewhere, Trina. Give Sara time to find him."

A tear slipped from one eye, and she ignored it like an unwelcome visitor. "Where will I have to go now?"

He led her to the leather couch. "You don't have to go anywhere, you know. You have a place right here."

Twin trails of tears now flowed down her cheeks. "What? What's here for me?"

Sam settled his legs onto the rough-hewn table in front of them. "Well, Trina, if you give that question some honest thought, I bet you'll come up with an answer."

She spent the night and the next day at his house. They did all the homey, mundane sorts of things couples do—watched baseball on TV and made love. Shared the Sunday paper and a shower. Trina even tried a couple of recipes from her mother's cookbook, and Sam tidied up the mess. By Sunday evening, she still didn't have the answer.

Was it because she needed him to give it to her in words? Or did he need her to say it first? Either way, they had reached a stalemate.

Sam took Trina back to her room at the lodge late that night, because she insisted. He left her with an admonishment. "Trina, once before I told you to think long and hard about where we were going. You went with your instincts then. Don't be afraid to trust them now."

Her instincts clamored for her to tie him down and scream "I love you" as many times, as many ways as she could think of.

Self-protection sent her into full retreat. "Right now I'm not sure I trust anything."

Trina spent all week firming up the final details for the Chimera expansion financing. She had worked out a joint-venture deal with two conservative lending institutions, and Sam had not only approved, he'd been pleased.

She'd kept her word to him, completing the job. Now she was free to go. To where? Sam had told her last weekend she didn't have to go anywhere, that she had a place here. But what would she do now that her work was finished?

Trina knew she wasn't the type of woman who could just hang around on the fringes, waiting for whatever attention a man decided to pay her. Even if she loved the man.

Knowing that she loved Sam but being afraid to

tell him because she feared he didn't love her in return made her almost as miserable as the indecision regarding her future. Something had to give soon. She couldn't survive many more days of uncertainty.

On Saturday she went to the monthly meeting of a businesswomen's association. Right after her arrival at the lake, she'd discovered that a local affiliate of the organization she'd belonged to in New York met at Chimera. She had started attending because the group gave her a renewed sense of identity and purpose. She'd met quite a few people that way and had hit it off well with several of the women who'd become friends over the course of the summer.

When the meeting adjourned, Sam was outside waiting for her. "Trina, Sara just called from Oregon. You'd better come talk to her."

Nine

Sam pivoted on one booted heel and started back, long strides chewing up the distance. Willing her rubbery legs into action, Trina scrambled to keep apace. It finally sank in that he was deliberately outdistancing her, so she gave up trying to catch him.

Disjointed questions rattled around inside her head, but her throat was so clogged she couldn't voice them.

Was there a chance Sara had located Tony? She cautioned herself against getting her hopes up too high, as she'd done with the earlier lead. The ensuing disappointment had devastated her.

Trina had never broken down so completely as she had the night when Sara called to report that the California connection hadn't panned out. Sam's calm reassurance had been the only thing standing between her and hysteria.

Speeding up, she vowed never to repeat that

outburst of excess emotions. This time, whatever turn the investigation had taken, she would accept it with poise.

When she entered Sam's office, she discovered it empty. Maybe he'd taken a detour to allow her privacy for the call. Or he didn't care to hear what Sara had discovered. Then again, he might want to spare himself another bout of Trina's irrational raving.

With tremulous hands she picked up the pink message slip, then began dialing the number. The five-zero-three area code didn't sound familiar, but she'd soon find out where the trail had led Sara this time. Ordering herself not to be optimistic was much easier than doing the deed.

Sara answered after the first ring, a crisp, businesslike greeting that drew a smile out of Trina, despite her nervousness. "Sam just relayed your message. Do you have some news?"

"Indeed I do. I followed a promising lead to a small town on the Oregon coast. I'm ninety-nine percent certain the man I traced here is your brother."

Trina leaped to her feet and immediately collapsed back in the chair. "Y-you did? You are? He is?"

She heard the smile in Sara's voice. "Yes, I believe this one is your Tony."

"Tony." Trina blinked back the sudden mist of tears. "After all this time. I can hardly believe it."

"You must feel overwhelmed about now. Would you like to take a while to absorb this? We can talk more later," Sara offered in her best grandmother's tone.

"No, no. I want to know everything now. Have you seen him? Is he healthy? Handsome?" How ridiculous! What did his looks matter if he was really her brother? She supposed the question had been sparked by years of envisioning him through the eyes of an adoring little sister.

"So far, I've only observed him from a distance since I didn't want to attempt contacting him until you gave me the go-ahead." She chuckled. "And yes, he looks quite fit and handsome."

Trina cross-examined Sara for another fifteen minutes until she was satisfied she'd gleaned every tidbit the investigation had yielded. Then she hung up, promising to get back to Sara as soon as possible with the details of her travel arrangements.

She remained seated another minute, eyes closed, mouthing a short prayer of thanks. After fifteen years it now came down to hours. Very soon she would see her brother again, face-to-face.

Sam! He had set the wheels in motion, and she was bursting to share the good news with him. A sense of *déjà vu* engulfed her when a clerk at the front desk sent her to accounting, whereupon they directed her to the marketing department. No Sam.

The late afternoon sun blinded her as she rushed from the main building back down the hill to the marina. There, a gas-pumping attendant told her Sam had taken off in his boat about ten minutes earlier.

"Damn the man," she fumed. Why had he run

away, knowing she'd want to tell him all about her conversation with Sara?

It took another half hour to claim her car and negotiate the twisting route to Sam's house. At least she'd driven it often enough not to get lost this time. She finally ran him to ground on his deck overlooking the lake, a beer bottle in his hands.

"I've never seen you drink," she said, so startled she momentarily forgot why she'd come.

He shrugged and downed a healthy swig. "I put away a fair amount in my younger days. Got it out of my system, I guess. Don't seem to need it anymore."

Trina eyed the overturned empty longneck on the planking beside his chair. "Do you think you need it today?"

He jerked his feet off the railing; the chair's front legs crashed to the deck. "Something tells me I may need a lot of it before the night's over."

As he got to his feet, towering over her, Trina was again reminded of their first encounter. Sam wasn't any more hospitable now than he'd been that day. And like then, she retreated a step.

"Sara's found Tony," she blurted out. "At least she's fairly certain it's him."

"So she told me."

When he didn't press for further details, Trina rushed to fill the gap. "He lives in a small town in Oregon where he's a building contractor. He's been married for eight years, and they have two children. Their house overlooks the ocean. I know how much Tony loves that."

She laced her fingers together, holding them in

front of her breasts. "Just think, Sam. I'm an aunt and a sister-in-law. Aunt Trina. I can't wait to buy them all kinds of presents and plan trips to the zoo."

When he still didn't comment, just kept piercing her with those laserlike green eyes, she slapped her hands on her hipbones. "Well, let's not get overly ecstatic here. After all, this only happens to be the most fantastic gift I've received in years. And you just stand there like the great stoneface."

"I might show more enthusiasm if I didn't have to worry about the other shoe falling."

"What do you mean?"

"I mean that now you've received this 'fantastic gift,' what's the next step? What do you plan to do about it?"

There could be only one answer, so obvious, she was incredulous that Sam had asked the question in the first place. "I'm flying out there, of course. On the first plane going that direction."

"Have you thought about calling Tony before you go? How can you be sure you'll get the reception you're hoping for if you just appear out of the blue?"

"He'll want to see me," Trina insisted stubbornly, though a niggle of doubt plagued her. "I'm his only family."

He slid open the glass door, leaving her to follow him inside. Getting another beer seemed to be his primary concern. "Correction," he said over his shoulder. "He's *your* only family. Tony already has one of his own. He made it himself."

Trina sucked in her breath at the implication. It was a low blow, doubly painful because Sam dealt it. The considerate, supportive friend and lover he'd been in St. Louis and since had vanished, replaced by this insensitive stranger. "You're being intentionally cruel. Why?"

"Because I don't want you to go." He gave the refrigerator door a violent slam and swung around. "Is that plain enough for you?"

When Trina saw the anguish in his eyes, she wrapped her arms around her, as if she could absorb his suffering and contain it. "This can't come as a surprise. I've never deceived you, never given any indication that it wouldn't come to this." A simple truth shouldn't inflict this much pain on either of them. "I'm sorry."

"Would it matter if I said I love you?"

Here was what she'd longed to hear, but coming now, she couldn't rejoice in it. "It matters, but it wouldn't stop me."

"Then I guess the only thing that might hold you here is if you loved me."

"I do love you." She'd never said it, but the emotional commitment to him had been a part of her for a long time. "I just can't let it keep me from carrying through with what I set out to do."

He slammed the unopened beer on the countertop. Trina winced at the sound of ceramic cracking. "Then tell me, Kat-a-rina, what am I supposed to do with this love of mine that matters so much you can walk away from it?"

She approached him, one hand on his forearm, hoping that the physical connection would comfort them both. "I don't have the answer to that yet, Sam. I haven't had the chance to think it through. Will you give me the time?"

His hands clamped over hers, so hard it hurt. "What are my other choices, Trina?"

She didn't have an answer to that, either.

Sam glanced at the red digital readout on his nightstand clock. One-fifteen. He'd been lying here wide-eyed for less than an hour. It seemed like a lifetime.

A foot away—it might as well have been a continent—Trina slept, though restlessly.

He'd finally got himself under control and thinking rationally enough to convince her it was useless to tear off to the local airport tonight. By the time she caught a commuter to St. Louis, she'd have missed the last flight to Portland and would have to stay overnight.

Then he had prevailed upon his staff to arrange the most convenient connections for her tomorrow. From outward appearances he'd played the part of a competent, take-charge executive.

Inside, he churned with anger and resentment and, tough to admit, pure terror.

He didn't want to let her go.

Trina's whole body twitched, and she turned to face the opposite wall. It was a tribute to his persuasiveness that she was here at all, so close that with a slight movement of his hand, he could touch her. And so far away that he didn't dare risk it.

If she was vulnerable, he was no less so. For years he'd zealously guarded himself against this kind of desolation. In the crunch all that wariness hadn't meant squat. Eyes wide open, he'd fallen, once again a victim of his accursed poor judgment of the opposite sex.

Sam's thoughts drifted back to her room at the lodge, where he'd watched her pack the items she couldn't live without, even temporarily. The odd assortment probably revealed everything he needed to know about Trina and what her quest was all about.

A small porcelain clock, lovingly wrapped, a worn looseleaf binder, its pages yellowed, a single forty-five record that produced a wistful smile and a sheen in her eyes. And those weird cans—soup and STP and foot powder—that were never far from her side. Those were the sparse remnants of her past with which she hoped to build a future. Her earnest hopefulness had squeezed his heart.

But she was going to leave him in the morning.

"Aw, to hell with it." He reached out and scooped Trina into the security of his arms. Unresisting, she murmured something he couldn't understand, and snuggled against him.

When dawn came, he'd slept a little in fits and starts, a great way to begin a day that had to rank as one of his all-time worsts.

"Sam?"

Her soft voice startled him. He hadn't yet psyched himself up to the level where he could bring off the departure scene without making a fool of himself. "You don't need to get up for another hour. Better grab all the sleep you can. It'll be a long day."

Her hand had been looped around his waist. She smoothed it over his chest. Again. "I'd rather make love."

He lay as stiff as a post, pleading for his traitorous body to deny her.

"I know you didn't want to last night, but I hope you'll feel differently this morning."

Didn't want to! Hell! He'd spent the night in agony because he had never wanted anything more. "I just don't think it would be in our best interests at this point, Trina." Real slick, Wonder. Make it sound like a business decision.

She apparently didn't intend to listen anyway. In the weeks they'd been together, Trina had learned him well. She knew where and how to touch, the moves that aroused him to fever pitch, and the words guaranteed to drive him wild. Without reservation she used every trick to wear down his resistance.

Except he didn't feel as if he were being tricked or used. He was being loved with everything she had, everything she was, and it was too powerful to fight.

They came together, fast, hard, desperate, and it ended in a fiery plunge to oblivion, granting them release but not satisfaction. Trina's tears dampened his face, but Sam couldn't swear all the moisture had come from her eyes.

Several hours later he put her on her flight. "I know I have to let you go, Trina. All I can hope is that love is strong enough to bring you back."

He could see the pain in her eyes, and she wasn't able to say anything. Sam could tell tears were again threatening when she walked up the steps to board.

Watching the small plane taxi, then speed down the runway and into the sky, he congratulated himself on his little farewell speech. Hell, that kind of tortured nobility had to elevate him to martyr status.

The plane disappeared into a cloudless midwestern sky, so blue it caused Sam's eyes to burn. A short, vicious expletive escaped through gritted teeth, clarifying his true opinion of nobility and martyrdom.

Sara had driven to Portland to meet Trina's plane. She was grateful for the other woman's consideration and support. It seemed unjust that what ought to have been one of the happiest days of her life was clouded by such numbing sadness.

"Thank you for staying over, Sara, and for coming here to pick me up. This has been a travel marathon," she said as they waited at baggage claim.

"All part of the service."

"I doubt that, but, nevertheless, I'm grateful." Sara's "service" was yet another reminder of Sam, as if she weren't burdened with far too many already.

If Sara noticed any sign of Trina's abstraction, she pretended not to. "I thought we'd stop for an early dinner and discuss your options for making initial contact with Tony."

Trina heard herself laugh self-consciously. "You can't imagine how many of those I've come up with and discarded during the trip. I want our reunion to be perfect, and yet I can think of so many reasons why it won't be."

"It's normal to be nervous in cases like this."

She gave Trina's hand a maternal pat. "Trust me, everything will turn out just fine."

In the end she saw no alternative but to defer to Sara's expertise and past experience. First thing Monday morning Sara would phone and make an appointment for herself at Tony's office. Then she would briefly summarize the situation and bring Trina in.

In theory it sounded like the ideal solution. In reality Trina was scared spitless as she sat awaiting her fate the next afternoon in the reception area of Tony's contracting firm.

What if Sara had made a mistake, and this Anthony Bartok wasn't her brother at all? Or suppose he was but didn't want to have anything to do with her? He might even get furious and kick her out or call the police to do it for him. She'd wind up being fingerprinted, having a mug shot taken . . .

Sara had been gone no more than a couple of minutes, and Trina had turned into a basket case. She didn't know how much longer she could endure the suspense. Tension had her so tied in knots, she barely noticed the door flying open.

"Sis?"

Yanked from her internal doomsaying, Trina started, peering up at the tall man dressed in jeans and a plaid shirt. If anything, the years had enhanced his good looks, and his body had filled out to match his height. "Tony? Oh, Tony, it *is* you!" She catapulted out of her seat, launching herself at him without contemplating how he might receive her.

She crashed into him with such force it propelled them backward a few steps before he could recover and steady them. Then the dam burst. She was laughing and crying and babbling nonsense even she couldn't understand. But it was okay, just as Sara had promised.

She'd found Tony.

Trina had to give him points for composure. He weathered the tempest stoically until she calmed down enough to start making sense. "I still can't believe it. I'd hoped and tried to be confident, but it was such a long shot."

He led her back into his office, and Sara excused herself, saying she would go back to the bed-and-breakfast where they'd spent last night, and wait to hear from Trina.

Rather than sit behind his big, cluttered desk, Tony took the chair beside her in front of it. "It's hard for me to believe that you tracked me here. How long has your detective been searching?"

Trina couldn't stop looking at him. "Only a few weeks, actually. Someone assured me that Sara was the best. I'm sitting next to the proof of it."

"You flew out from New York yesterday?"

That, of course, made her think of Sam. "No. It's a long story that I'll fill you in on later. First I want to hear about you." She waved a hand at his desk. "Your business. Your family."

"The company is small, but it was never my intention to build an empire. I'm just thankful I can make a living doing something I like." He held his palms out to her, the calluses visible. "I never could buy Papa's propaganda about not working with our hands. What's so bad about it if that's what makes you happy?"

"You are, aren't you, Tony? Happy?"

"Thanks to my family." He stretched to pluck a picture frame off his desk. "My wife's name is Eve. We were married eight years ago. Eric is six and will be starting school this fall. The little one is Amy, who unfortunately has already learned to manipulate Daddy in the way only four-year-old daughters can."

Trina brought the photograph close to her because her eyes had clouded up again. She had shed so many tears in the past two days, she must have exhausted a lifetime's supply. "They're precious, all of them."

"I had just started on my own when I met Eve. She's been my partner in all ways from the very first." His voice was laden with emotion. "I wasn't looking for what I found with my family, had no idea it even existed. My history in that area didn't exactly make me great husband and father material. But I took one look at Eve, and that was it for me. Boom! It was like magic. I knew I'd do whatever it took to have her."

Trina recalled her first impression of Sam and had to blink back another spell of crying. What was wrong with her? Tears of happiness were one thing. This was unreasonable. Did everything that occurred have to trigger memories of Sam? "So many times I've wondered and worried about you, hoped your life had turned out the way you wanted it to."

"I've thought about you a lot, too, Sis. Even after Papa said you hated me for what I'd done to Mama and that you never wanted to see me again."

The room tipped out of focus. Trina's ears rang. "What? Papa told you that? When?"

Tony crossed his arms over his chest, as if to protect himself. "Over six years ago, soon after Eric was born. I'd gotten my act together by then, and wanted him to know he had a grandson."

Elbow on the chair arm, Trina propped her forehead on one hand. "This is unbelievable. He never said one word to me. I had no idea you'd tried to get in touch. How could he have been so cold and cruel to both of us? There has never been a day in my life when I didn't want to see you."

She massaged her temple. "I knew he was rigid, unfair, but I never imagined he could be so spiteful and vindictive. It's just incredible."

"He said Mama had died, and it was all my fault. That she'd never been the same since I ran away—like a common thief, as he phrased it."

"Oh, Tony," she said, touching his arm. "Mama mourned and missed you. You were her firstborn. But your leaving certainly didn't cause her death. Lord, how awful for you having to live with such a hateful accusation. He tried to pile that guilt on you because he didn't know who else to blame. I'm sorry."

"That's another way Eve's helped me. She worked as a counselor before Eric's birth. I have to admit there have been quite a few problems I needed to deal with. Luckily she's stood by me all the way. I'm in pretty good shape, I think, because I've learned to focus on the areas of my life I can control, and to let go of those I can't."

"She sounds like a treasure."

"To me, she's that and more. In fact, I think the

two of you will get along very well. She's an only child, and has always wanted a big sister."

Trina's heart swelled with happiness and pride and a wealth of other feelings too new to name. "I can't wait."

Late that afternoon Trina sat on the terrace overlooking the Pacific. Tony had dropped her back at the bed-and-breakfast several hours earlier, on his way home to tell the family about Trina's unexpected appearance. He and Eve would be by later to take her out to a celebration dinner. Later she would return home with them.

She had a family. At last. In her wildest dreams she couldn't have planned a better reception. It amazed her that Tony could welcome her so warmly after years of assuming *she* was the one who'd wanted the ties severed permanently.

Shaking her head, she pressed her fingers to her lips. What monstrous flaw in her father had driven him to turn his back on his child and grandchild? What warped sense of right and wrong had made it justifiable to keep Tony's call a secret? Trina wondered if she'd ever known Anton Bartok at all.

How fortunate that Tony had had the good sense to escape when he had, and to emerge from their father's tyranny relatively unscathed. Apart from the obvious issue of control, did she bear scars that she wasn't aware of?

A vivid orange explosion of sunset made the ocean look almost black in contrast. The sunsets she'd watched from Sam's deck were softer, muted by the trees that screened the horizon. It would already be dark in the Ozarks. Was he sitting on the deck thinking of her, speculating about how her day had gone?

Suddenly she knew she couldn't wait to talk to him. She needed to share her good news, needed simply to hear his voice. After hurrying to her room, she punched out the number, impatient with the slightest delay.

It took six rings before he picked up. "Wonder."

It never changed. One word from him, and her heart was off and running. "Sam, it's me. Trina." She held her breath at the pause.

"Are you all right?"

The breath trickled out on a wave of relief. He'd been concerned about her, a good sign. "I'm fine. Wonderful, in fact." She filled him in on all she'd learned, which was only the tip of the iceberg, but still a remarkable beginning.

"It sounds as though it went down smooth as silk. The bottom line looks good, then?"

Trina scowled at the receiver. Sam never talked in clichés. "Everything here looks good," she conceded, feeling a little less animated than a moment ago. "How's everything there?"

"What can I say? I'm here in my little heaven and all's right with the world."

That told her nothing, plus she didn't care for the flat way he'd recited the words. "But how are *you*?"

"What do you want, Trina? For me to bleed all over the phone? Tell you I'm wasting away for lack of your love? That I don't even want to eat anymore? Or how about that I drank a half-bottle of scotch last night and got blind drunk for the first time in my life? Is that the kind of stuff that interests you?"

"No, that's precisely the kind of stuff I don't want to hear. I can't picture you doing any of it."

"It's the truth, every last sordid detail. And if I didn't feel so stinking lousy, I'd have already started working my way through the rest of that scotch."

She clutched the phone so tightly, her knuckles turned white. "Sam, this isn't like you at all. What do you hope to accomplish by going off the deep end this way?"

He laughed, a sharp sound that chilled her. "How about a good night's sleep, Kat-a-rina? Or a few minutes peace when my hands don't itch to touch you? That's what I'm trying to accomplish. Any other questions?"

"No." No questions, but if she'd thought a stern lecture would do any good, she'd deliver one worth remembering. She paced a path restricted by the length of the phone cord.

"Then I have one for you. When are you ever going to find time to think about me? About us?"

Sam and the distance separating them were never far from her mind. She was so torn, wanting to be with her family while at the same time yearning to be close to the man she loved. "I am thinking about you. Why else would I have called?"

He took quite a while to think that over. "I'm not sure. Why don't you tell me?"

Trina knew what he was asking, what he needed to hear. "I called because I care, even if I'm not there to show you. And because I love you."

"Well, thank God you haven't forgotten that, at least."

That sounded more like her Sam. She heard the clink of ice striking glass. "Sam, don't you dare pick up that scotch bottle. I mean it! Are you listening to me?"

He chuckled. "Yes, honey. Is it all right if I pour myself a mug of limeade?"

She pursed her lips. "You're not just saying that to make me shut up, are you?"

"I never knew you had this tendency to nag. Practicing to be a mother?"

A familiar heat flooded Trina. She dropped to the bed. A mother. Naturally she'd thought about having children in the abstract, as a possibility for the future. Her feelings for Sam made her think in far more specific and immediate terms. But more than a half-continent was keeping them apart. By his own admission Sam had been happily single for ten years. He'd said nothing to indicate he was willing to change his status and make a commitment to her.

"Practicing for my niece and nephew, maybe. Just think, I'm an aunt. The little girl, Amy—her middle name is Katarina. They named her after me. I was so touched. And I can't wait to meet her and Eric. Tony had a picture. They're so beautiful." As Sam's children would be. She warned herself not to dwell on that. When he'd spoken of Robert's desire for grandchildren, it was with disdain, as if he wanted no part of it.

"I might not have sounded like it earlier, Trina, but I am glad you found what you were looking for."

"Everything I'd hoped for, and more."

"There's only one thing I want to add. I hope you'll soon realize that everything and more is not enough."

Ten

A week later Trina stood on the windswept bank overlooking the ocean. She'd got in the habit of coming here several times a day to think. Tony had always been a water lover. Why had she never shared his fascination with it? At the Ozarks and now here she'd sampled its calming and therapeutic powers. Like Shobi's little hidden garden, it encouraged introspection.

Invariably she dredged up the parting words of her phone conversation with Sam. He had sown the seed of doubt with his suggestion that her newfound family might not be enough. She wanted to hold him responsible, somehow, that it was turning out as he'd predicted.

Oh, she was happy being with Tony and Eve, and enjoyed getting to know her niece and nephew. But the restlessness that had permeated her life since she'd set out cross-country, and even before that, hadn't disappeared.

She couldn't continue imposing on her brother's hospitality. Even the most desirable guests eventually wore out their welcome. Trina pitched in as much as she could, but this wasn't her home, and that became increasingly apparent with each day.

Where to go? The town was charming, but small. There weren't any jobs for somebody in her field. She could go to California as originally planned, though she had no real reason to settle there now.

She stuffed her hands into the deep pockets of her windbreaker. With the afternoon sun buried in cloudbanks, the wind chilled. Trina craved warmth in July.

That brought Sam to mind, as almost everything did. It was warm where he was, but that had nothing to do with the heat he generated from within. She tunneled her hands inside her sleeves and massaged the goose bumps.

Sam would never have to worry about where to go. He'd staked out his territory, built it according to his vision, and planned to stay there forever. How Trina longed to possess that absolute certainty of place and future.

That was what her life lacked, what Sam had told her she would have to make for herself. Had she truly been so naive as to believe the answer lay in finding Tony? Knowing her brother and his family would be a part of her life from now on was comforting; it filled some of the empty spaces.

But it was not enough.

For some time now the realization had been floating through her consciousness, building, clarifying. She wanted it all—Sam and a marriage proposal and everything else that went along with being husband and wife, including a family of her own.

The major obstacle might turn out to be what she desired most. Sam. So independent and self-contained, so confident he had everything he needed. Could he possibly love her enough to make a real place for her in his future?

Trina didn't doubt that he wanted her with him. But for how long? He'd told her he was a one-woman man, and she believed that. Had he meant forever?

There was only one sure way to find out. Go back and ask. And if Sam didn't give her the answers she wanted to hear, then she'd just have to dig in and fight until he saw things her way.

A storm was rolling in off the Pacific, darkening the clouds, whipping the wind harder against her. She'd have to go in soon, knowing the rain would depress her, make her yearn for Sam. But first thing in the morning she'd take steps to ease at least part of the yearning.

"Kat-a-rina?"

She shook her head, telling herself it must be a hallucination, born of the need to hear Sam's voice. Indeed, it rose up inside her, powerful and unrelenting like the waves striking the shoreline below.

She would go in, and she would call him. Right now! She would talk to him for as long as the storm lasted and hope it might hold the despair at bay.

And then she would make plans.

Trina whirled around . . . and collided with six feet four inches of hard man. "Sam?"

"In the flesh."

She plastered herself to him, touching him everywhere she could reach, as fast as she could reach. "It's really you. For a second I thought you had to be a phantom, straight out of my daydreams."

"That's a good start, telling me I was on your mind." His arms tighten around her. "Now, do you think you might make the welcome a little more personalized?"

"You mean like this?" She framed his face, bringing his mouth to hers for a long, deep joining that was rife with affirmation.

"You haven't lost your touch," he said, his lips moving against hers. "That better not be because you've been practicing."

She traded wry smiles with him. "I know this will swell your ego disgracefully, but I can't imagine kissing another man. Ever!"

He grinned. It did interesting things to his sharply defined features and insidious things to her equilibrium. "Well, honey, that ought to dovetail just fine with what I have in mind. Which is why I chased you to the edge of the earth."

The first raindrops blew in off the water before he could explain the reason for his trip. Hand in hand they ran for the house, but the storm moved faster than they did. Damp and shivering, they huddled inside the French doors of the breakfast room.

"I'll get us some towels," Trina offered, not wanting to spare the time away from Sam to change into dry clothes. "Then I want to hear why you chased me to the edge of the earth."

She returned with two bathsheets. "Eve and the kids don't seem to be anywhere around. It's odd that they just disappeared."

Sam blotted his face and arms. "When I showed up at the door and introduced myself, she got a knowing look in her eye. Probably suspects what brought me here. Anyway, she got a brainstorm to take Eric and Amy to a matinee, then meet Tony and have dinner out."

"Very convenient of her to come up with that idea." Trina filled the kettle with water and set it on the burner, then spooned loose tea into a flowered pot. "How about letting me in on what you think Eve suspects?"

"Well, I think it'll work out better if you come over here and sit down so I can see you when I say my speech."

"Goodness, this sounds serious. Let me take care of our snack first. I might need fortification, and you always do."

She bustled about setting out cups, saucers, and dessert plates. Then she unwrapped some of the pastry she and Eve had made that morning. At last she had it all arranged to her satisfaction on the breakfast table. "Okay, shoot."

Sam took a swallow of tea and winced. He touched the tip of his tongue experimentally. "Off to a good start."

"Is this really so hard to say?"

"Well, yeah, kinda. It's the first time I've ever done this, so I hope I get it right."

Trina smiled and reached out to grasp his hand.

"You're rarely at a loss for words, so I'm sure you'll do fine."

His fingers flexed. "Okay, here goes. Trina Bartok, I love you. You already know that, but I'm taking it a step further. I want to marry you, share my home with you, and before long, get busy making those little Wonders Dad's been pressuring me about."

Bubbling with enthusiasm, she opened her mouth, not knowing for sure what she planned to say. He shushed her before she could speak. "I'll be a low-maintenance kind of husband. Housekeeping from the lodge takes care of cleaning my house, the laundry keeps my clothes clean, and I eat most meals there, as you know. There's no reason any of that has to change. I want a wife, not maid service."

He held up a hand when she would have interrupted. "We have already proven we're a good working team. We'll just expand your job description. In addition to a wife, I'll be getting a business partner, unless you decide you want to do something else, which will be okay with me, as long as you're happy.

"You've made friends at the lodge and with some of the people in the area. My family is crazy about you, so there isn't any question of your fitting right in. You've already made a place for yourself in their hearts."

Trina felt the familiar sting of tears, but these were brought on by happiness. "Oh, Sam, I—"

"Don't stop me now. Unless I get this all out at once, I might lose momentum. Now, I know I spouted that poetic nonsense about letting you go, that if it's meant to be, you'd come back to me." His eyes drilled into hers. "That's a bunch of crap, Trina."

Sam jumped up, bracing one arm against the door frame. "Maybe it was wise to give you some time and distance, but there's a limit. I'm not the kind of man who leaves anything to chance, especially not something this important. That's why I've come all this way. To take you back with me."

His posture—legs spread, hands planted on his hips, head thrust forward—screamed confrontation. "I know how much you wanted to find your brother. You did, and that's good. I don't care how many times a year you want to visit them out here. They can bring the kids to the lake, too, whenever they want. But I'm not going to stand by and let you live on secondhand happiness. Not when I can give you the genuine article."

He leaned forward, looking even more intimidating. "Now if I can break a ten-year pattern and let a woman back into my life, you can damn well take this proposal seriously."

He stopped to drag in a breath, and Trina pounced on her first chance to get a word in. "One question. Do I have a say in this at all?"

Wary now, he dropped his fisted hands to his side. "Depends."

She rose and approached him. "Depends on what?"

"On whether you say the right thing."

"Fair enough. How does this sound?" Trina captured one of his hands and unfolded the stiff fingers, then laid her palm against his. "The happiest I've ever been was the time I spent with you in the Ozarks."

His fingers folded to twine with hers. "I like what I'm hearing already. Go on."

"You were right all along about my needing to build my own happiness. Luckily I have a good teacher, who, by the way, will also make a fantastic business partner, father, and husband. Have I left anything out?"

"Sounds pretty near perfect to me," Sam said in that hoarse voice she had loved since the first time she'd heard it.

He was now hugging her so tightly she could barely get out the most important words of all. "Yes. Yes, to everything. I love you."

A song played inside her head. Trina heard the echo of her mother's words and smiled. She'd found her very own "Mr. Wonderful."

Epilogue

Trina braced her hands on the deck railing and faced the first golden rays of sunrise striking the lake surface. She never got tired of the view from here, not even in winter. Each day brought with it subtle variations, but there was a constancy, too, that she could always count on. In fact, she had begun to think of the lake as a metaphor for the life she'd found here.

She felt Sam's warmth a second before his arms stole around her waist and nestled her back in the cradle of his chest. They shared sunrise this way almost every morning, another constant Trina had grown to cherish and rely on.

"You should have rested a little more today. It's going to be a long one, and once we get to the lodge, it'll be nonstop."

Trina smoothed her hands along his bare forearms. "I know. I woke up an hour ago and was too excited to go back to sleep. This is my first Memorial Day as one of the family. The opening of our first full season together."

She felt Sam inhale deeply. "It's going to be the best year ever, Trina." Fingers spread, his hands spanned her stomach. "I can feel it."

Trina nodded, then a small laugh shook her. "I guess Robert will really be feeling smug when we tell him our news tonight. First he got me the job. Then he got his only child married. Now he's going to get his grandchild for a Christmas present."

"Yep, the old meddler has gotten everything he wanted." Gently Sam brought her around to face him, kissing her with reverence and enough love to sustain her a lifetime. "But he can't be any happier than I am. 'Cause I have everything I want too."

THE EDITOR'S CORNER

What could be more romantic than weddings? Picture the bride in an exquisite gown. Imagine the handsome groom in a finely tailored tuxedo. Hear them promise "to have and to hold" each other forever. This is the perfect ending to courtship, the joyous ritual we cherish in our hearts. And next month, in honor of June brides, we present six fabulous LOVESWEPTs with beautiful brides and handsome grooms on the covers.

Leading the line-up is **HER VERY OWN BUTLER**, LOVESWEPT #552, another sure-to-please romance from Helen Mittermeyer. Single mom Drew Laughlin wanted a butler to help run her household, but she never expected a muscled, bronzed Hercules to apply. Rex Dakeland promised an old friend to check up on Drew and her children, but keeping his secret soon feels too much like spying. Once unexpected love ensnares them both, could he win her trust and be her one and only? A real treat, from one of romance's best-loved authors.

Gail Douglas pulls out all the stops in **ALL THE WAY**, LOVESWEPT #553. Jake Mallory and Brittany Thomas shared one fabulous night together, but he couldn't convince her it was enough to build their future on. Now, six months later, Jake is back from his restless wandering and sets out to prove to Brittany that he's right. It'll take fiery kisses and spellbinding charm to make her believe that the reckless nomad is finally ready to put down roots. Gail will win you over with this charming love story.

WHERE THERE'S A WILL . . . by Victoria Leigh, LOVESWEPT #554, is a sheer delight. Maggie Cooper plays a ditzy seductress on the ski slopes, only to prove to herself that she's sexy enough to kindle a man's desire. And boy, does she kindle Will Jackson's desire! He usually likes to do the hunting, but letting Maggie work her wiles on him is tantalizing fun. And after he's freed her from her doubts, he'll teach her to dare to love. There's a lot of wonderful verve and dash in this romance from talented Victoria.

Laura Taylor presents a very moving, very emotional love story in **DESERT ROSE**, LOVESWEPT #555. Emma Hamilton and David Winslow are strangers caught in a desperate situation, wrongfully imprisoned in a foreign country. Locked in adjacent cells, they whisper comfort to each other and reach through iron bars to touch hands. Love blossoms between them in that dark prison, a love strong enough to survive until fate finally brings them freedom. You'll cry and cheer for these memorable lovers. Bravo, Laura!

There's no better way to describe Deacon Brody than **RASCAL,** Charlotte Hughes's new LOVESWEPT, #556. He was once a country-music sensation, and he's never forgotten how hard he struggled to make it—or the woman who broke his heart. Losing Cody Sherwood sends him to Nashville determined to make her sorry she let him go, but when he sees her again, he realizes he's never stopped wanting her or the passion that burned so sweetly between them. Charlotte delivers this story with force and fire.

Please give a rousing welcome to Bonnie Pega and her first novel, **ONLY YOU,** LOVESWEPT #557. To efficiency expert Max Shore, organizing Caitlin Love's messy office is a snap compared to uncovering the sensual woman beneath her professional facade. A past pain has etched caution deep in her heart, and only Max can show her how to love again. This enchanting novel will show you why we're excited to have Bonnie writing for LOVESWEPT. Enjoy one of our New Faces of '92!

On sale this month from FANFARE are three marvelous novels. The historical romance **HEATHER AND VELVET** showcases the exciting talent of a rising star—Teresa Medeiros. Her marvelous touch for creating memorable characters and her exquisite feel for portraying passion and emotion shine in this grand adventure of love between a bookish orphan and a notorious highwayman known as the Dreadful Scot Bandit. Ranging from the storm-swept English countryside to the wild moors of Scotland, **HEATHER AND VELVET** has garnered the following praise from *New York Times* bestselling author Amanda Quick: "A terrific tale full of larger-than-life characters and thrilling romance." Teresa Medeiros—a name to watch for.

Lush, dramatic, and poignant, **LADY HELLFIRE** by Suzanne Robinson is an immensely thrilling historical romance. Its hero, Alexis de Granville, Marquess of Richfield, is a cold-blooded rogue whose tragic—and possibly violent—past has hardened his heart to love . . . until he melts at the fiery touch of Kate Grey's sensual embrace.

Anna Eberhardt, who writes short romances under the pseudonym Tiffany White, has been nominated for *Romantic Times*'s Career Achievement award for Most Sensual Romance in a series. In **WHISPERED HEAT**, she delivers a compelling contemporary novel of love lost, then regained. When Slader Reems is freed after five years of being wrongly imprisoned, he sets out to reclaim everything that was taken from him—including Lissa Jamison.

Also on sale this month, in the Doubleday hardcover edition, is **HIGHLAND FLAME** by Stephanie Bartlett, the stand-alone "sequel" to **HIGHLAND REBEL**. Catriona Galbaith, now a widow, is thrust into a new struggle—and the arms of a new love.

Happy reading!

With best wishes,

Nita Taublib

Nita Taublib
Associate Publisher
LOVESWEPT and FANFARE

FANFARE

On Sale in June

RAVISHED

☐ 29316-8 $4.99/5.99 in Canada
by Amanda Quick
<u>New York Times</u> bestselling author

Sweeping from a cozy seaside village to glittering London, this enthralling tale of a thoroughly mismatched couple poised to discover the rapture of love is Amanda Quick at her finest.

THE PRINCESS

☐ 29836-4 $5.99
by Celia Brayfield

He is His Royal Highness, the Prince Richard, and wayward son of the House of Windsor. He has known many women, but only three understand him, and only one holds the key to unlock the mysteries of his heart.

SOMETHING BLUE

☐ 29814-3 $5.99/6.99 in Canada
by Ann Hood
author of SOMEWHERE OFF THE COAST OF MAINE

"An engaging, warmly old fashioned story of the perils and endurance of romance, work, and friendship." -- <u>The Washington Post</u>

SOUTHERN NIGHTS

☐ 29815-1 $4.99/5.99 in Canada
by Sandra Chastain,
Helen Mittermeyer, and Patricia Potter

Sultry, caressing, magnolia-scented breezes. . .sudden, fierce thunderstorms. . .nights of beauty and enchantment. In three original novellas, favorite LOVESWEPT authors present the many faces of summer and unexpected love.

FANFARE

FANFARE

Rosanne Bittner

_____ 28599-8 EMBERS OF THE HEART . $4.50/5.50 in Canada
_____ 29033-9 IN THE SHADOW OF THE MOUNTAINS
$5.50/6.99 in Canada
_____ 28319-7 MONTANA WOMAN .... $4.50/5.50 in Canada
_____ 29014-2 SONG OF THE WOLF .... $4.99/5.99 in Canada

Deborah Smith

_____ 28759-1 THE BELOVED WOMAN .. $4.50/ 5.50 in Canada
_____ 29092-4 FOLLOW THE SUN .... $4.99/ 5.99 in Canada
_____ 29107-6 MIRACLE .... $4.50/ 5.50 in Canada

Tami Hoag

_____ 29053-3 MAGIC .... $3.99/4.99 in Canada

Dianne Edouard and Sandra Ware

_____ 28929-2 MORTAL SINS .... $4.99/5.99 in Canada

Kay Hooper

_____ 29256-0 THE MATCHMAKER, ... $4.50/5.50 in Canada
_____ 28953-5 STAR-CROSSED LOVERS .. $4.50/5.50 in Canada

Virginia Lynn

_____ 29257-9 CUTTER'S WOMAN, ... $4.50/4.50 in Canada
_____ 28622-6 RIVER'S DREAM, ... $3.95/4.95 in Canada

Patricia Potter

_____ 29071-1 LAWLESS .... $4.99/ 5.99 in Canada
_____ 29069-X RAINBOW .... $4.99/ 5.99 in Canada